MOSHIE CAT

Moshie Cat is the true story of a kitten in Majorca. Island life for Moshie Cat is a continuous cycle of ups and downs – frightening episodes and exciting discoveries. His explorations lead him to make many new friends, both human and feline. There is always something or someone new on Moshie Cat's horizon.

Helen Griffiths wrote her first children's book at the age of fifteen, and she has now written eleven books. Married to a Spaniard, she has lived in Lausanne, Majorca and Madrid, and she has three daughters.

HELEN GRIFFITHS

MOSHIE CAT

The true adventures of a Mallorquin kitten

Cover illustration by Alexy Pendle
Text illustrations by Shirley Hughes

A Piccolo Book

PAN BOOKS LTD
LONDON

First published 1969 by Hutchinson Junior Books Ltd.
This edition published 1972 by Pan Books Ltd,
33 Tothill Street, London, SW1.

ISBN 0 330 23263 0

Made and printed in Great Britain by
Cox & Wyman Ltd, London, Reading and Fakenham

CONTENTS

Mosh is the Mallorquin word for cat

Telling of Moshie Cat's birthplace
and something of his mother and father

Moshie Cat was born on a beautiful island, an island covered with hills and pine trees and heather and surrounded by a sea that is almost as blue as the sky.

He was born in a little village which straggles in triangular fashion in a valley at the bottom of a steep range of hills. The village is not far from the coast and from its highest streets the sea is plainly visible, shimmering silver in the sunlight, across a vista of orchards and isolated palm trees.

It is a village full of white or sand-brown houses with red roofs and green shutters. Each house has a small garden or a strip of orchard, and it was in one of these orchards that Moshie Cat was born.

In the orchard was an open shed which was both a pigsty and a corral for rabbits and pigeons. Between the two was a space where foodstuffs were stored and it was here, beneath a low stone shelf, in a broken wooden box, that Moshie Cat's mother put her litter of kittens.

There were only three. One was black and the other two were black-and-white.

One of the latter was very pretty, with perfect, uniform markings. Four white paws, a white chest and tummy, and a white blaze from head to nose.

The other was all higgledy-piggledy patches, black in the middle of the white stretches, white in the middle of the black, and instead of the pretty white blaze that most black-and-white cats have down the centre of their faces, he had a black one.

It was not even a perfect black face, for there was a white splash over his left eye and both his cheeks were white. In the middle of all this whiteness he had a black chin so that he really was the most higgledy-piggledy of black-and-white cats.

This, of course, was Moshie Cat.

He did not know that he was such an odd-looking kitten. All he knew when he was so very, very tiny was how warm his mother and sisters were and how delicious was the milk his mother gave him.

He did not even know that he was in a box, on a strip of blue blanket, under a shelf between the pig and the rabbits and pigeons. His eyes were lost in the blackness of his furrowed face; his ears were so tiny that they could hardly be seen, and the whole of him could fit easily into a person's hand.

In the first few days of his life he did no more than feel the closeness of his mother, cry when she was not there, and snuggle up tightly to her when she was.

He and his sisters had a very loud cry. It still was not a proper 'miau' nor even a mew. It was a wail, sharp and piercing, and it would bring back the mother cat from wherever she had wandered very quickly.

Moshie Cat's mother was beautiful. She was a dark tortoiseshell with orange eyes, very small and very timid, graceful in all her movements.

Her favourite haunt was the jungle of prickly-pear at the bottom of a neighbour's garden, at

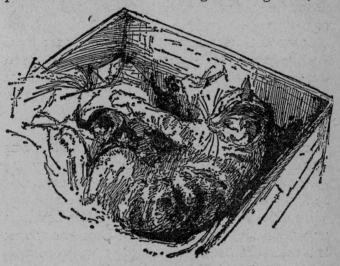

whose centre the sun could not reach. She would stretch out carefully among the prickles and doze for hours, safe from children and dogs.

Sometimes she dozed with her eyes open. There was something mystic about the bland orange depths. A person, seeing so steady and unblinking a gaze, would be forced to wonder what she was thinking about. Most probably she was thinking of nothing.

Her constant companion was a scruffy tramp of a cat, black and ugly, who had only one eye. He was her shadow. Wherever the Tortoiseshell went, he followed. Apart from his scruffiness and the lack of an eye, the only special thing about him was his devotion to the timid she-cat.

This ragged, scar-faced creature was Moshie Cat's father.

Moshie Cat never knew his father, for the Tortoiseshell would not let him near the old box under the shelf. The black cat would sit up on a ledge nearby and watch the baby rabbits hop about among the locust beans and dry bread. They made him feel very hungry.

He would have eaten them if he could but the owner of the rabbits knew this and had fenced the corral very firmly with fine wire netting. The rabbits could not get out and the cats could not get in.

Oddly enough, it never occurred to him that pigeons were edible and the fat, noisy birds flapped about at will in the orchard, able to return to their nest-boxes through the gap left at the top of the wire.

Sometimes the black cat would hear the kittens wailing for their mother. He would stare down from the ledge with his one good eye but he could not see them under the shelf. With a bored expression he would return his gaze to the rabbits. They were far more interesting, fluffy and quick and sweet-smelling.

Moshie Cat's mother took no interest in the rabbits. She knew that she must not touch them. But then, Moshie Cat's mother was lucky enough to have someone who fed her. It was only bones and scrapings from the plates, and sometimes the hard bread that was saved for the rabbits, but it was better than nothing.

Moshie Cat's father lived by what he could hunt or steal or scrounge from the rubbish bins, which was why he was so thin and had only one eye.

The three tiny kittens, curled up on the bit of blue blanket, did not know how lucky they were. They only knew the comfort of their mother's caressing tongue, the sweetness of her milk, and the warmth of her presence.

For them the rest of the world did not yet exist.

Describing Moshie Cat's world
and how he left it

When Moshie Cat and his sisters were ten days old they opened their eyes. All three had dark blue, wonder-filled eyes which as yet could see very little. They did not need to see much for still they were too tiny to venture from the box.

They could smell the pig and they could smell the rabbits and pigeons, but these smells meant little to them. The only thing they recognized was the smell of their mother.

They knew her voice too; her short, soft mews of greeting, her sharp yowl which terminated in a long growl when she was cross. The pig's squeals of hunger in the early morning, and her satisfied grunts and splashes when she was fed, were quite incomprehensible to them.

Perhaps they wondered too at the constantly billing pigeons. Only the rabbits were silent.

When one day a human neighbour came to see them, and picked them up one by one, they were very much afraid. They wailed in his hands and hurriedly wriggled back into the safety of each other when they were put down.

The mother cat came running to see why her babies cried. She drew back at the sight of the man,

afraid to venture farther in spite of her kittens'
need. She looked at the man with anxious orange
eyes and as soon as he moved away she carefully
fitted herself into the box beside them, covering
them with her warm orange-and-black flank.

The man said to the mother cat's mistress,
'There's a mouse in the larder. We could do with a
cat.'

They were not seen again until they were bigger
and more venturesome, almost three weeks old.
They had at last found the courage, or the curiosity, to clamber out from the box under the shelf
and were sitting in a patch of sunlight, warming
themselves, when the neighbour walked by.

The mother cat was stretched out nearby, watching them lazily. After a while they tired of sitting
still and began to play with their paws and each
other's tails.

They were very sweet, little black-and-white
things playing in the patterns of April sunshine, but
the neighbour did not notice that. He only remem-
bered the mouse that still visited his larder.

Moshie Cat and his sisters grew more venturesome. The orchard was an exciting, enticing world,
a jungle of melon trailers, sprawling artichokes and
sprouting cabbages.

They tangled themselves in leaves and roots,
fighting with flattened ears to escape. They
crouched among the furrows of the potato crop and
watched with whipping tails the birds that came to
peck at the soil and the fat pigeons strutting about
with red legs and yellow eyes.

Sometimes they wandered quite a long way from their mother, clambering among the pink and yellow roses that decorated the wire netting of the orchard's fence, or hiding among the dandelions and other wild flowers that grew thick on the borders.

It was a beautiful playground for the three small kittens, free from danger and full of teasing plants and shadows.

They no longer returned to the box to sleep but preferred to snuggle under the geraniums that grew against the wall of the pigsty. They spent the heat of the day among the cool green stalks of wild corn that also sprang up in thick patches.

All three were very, very wild.

The mother cat was always somewhere nearby for all that she left them alone, and the black tom-cat stalked about the orchard and watched the rabbits. The kittens stared at him and were afraid. He looked very fierce. They did not know that he was their father and would not harm them.

Such joy, however, was not to last. There came a time when Moshie Cat and his sisters wanted more than milk. They were sleek and round-tummied and full of energy. Their teeth were needle-sharp and they wanted solid food to chew on, preferably meat.

They were as hungry as three young tigers and there was nothing for them to eat.

With great patience Moshie Cat would fix his gaze upon a yellow butterfly, fluttering from flower to flower. At a pounce, he had it between his paws, only to find that the wings were thinner than a rose petal and the body the tiniest morsel of food.

His comical, cockeyed face drawn into a frown, he chewed the butterfly. In a minute he was hungry again.

Moshie Cat's tale might have ended very soon had it not been for the neighbour who had a mouse in his larder. The village was full of kittens like himself, belonging to and wanted by no one.

He and his sisters would have played until they could play no more; they would have hungered until they could hunger no more; and one day the orchard would have been tranquil again, the leaves still, without the movement of them.

As it was, all three of them found homes. The neighbour with the mouse had decided that, in return for the favour of a kitten, he would find homes for the others. Accordingly he carried off one to the butcher's wife who wanted a plaything for her daughters and another, the black one, to a couple of shoe-menders.

They were a lonely pair, with neither children nor grandchildren to keep them company. They were very pleased with the idea of a little cat and to this day she sleeps beside them on a chair, among the broken shoes.

The neighbour saved the tom-cat for himself. It looked the ugliest, but at least it could not have kittens.

Moshie Cat was on his own in the orchard for a few days. He stayed close to his mother and played with her tail. He was lonely without his sisters.

When the neighbour came to look for him he was not to be found. His mother had moved him to another part of the orchard and kept him hidden among the geraniums. There eventually he was discovered, kneading his mother's flank and taking from her the last milk that she would give him.

The Tortoiseshell looked up at the man with wise orange eyes and did nothing when Moshie Cat was picked up and carried, protesting, away.

In which Moshie Cat finds it
hard to survive

Rafael, Mari-Loli, Manolita and Tomasin were thrilled with the idea of a kitten in the house. Moshie Cat crouched on the broken-tiled floor, surrounded by their dirty faces and grasping hands. He was ready for flight and his tiny heart pounded with fear.

He dashed underneath the washing-machine and with a cry of delight they dragged him out again by the tail.

He escaped and fled to the insecure comfort of the darkness behind a curtain that hung down from the sink, but their eager hands found him there also and dragged him out by the scruff of the neck.

This time they did not let him go. First Rafael, then Mari-Loli and Manolita explored him from whiskers to tail, turning him upside down, holding him by a leg or his tail or nearly crushing his ribs, while Tomasin – the youngest – screeched for his turn too, and grabbed at a handful of fur whenever he could.

They did not mean to be cruel to him. They just could not imagine that a kitten might have any feelings.

Tomasin pulled his ears and whiskers; Rafael

pushed him inside his toy covered-waggon and took him for a ride; and the two girls dressed him up in their dolls' clothes, smacking him hard whenever he struggled.

After an hour or so of this Moshie Cat was still and let them do as they wished with his body. He

had forgotten that his beautiful playground had once existed and that he had been happy there.

His world now was one of uncaring hands and endless shoutings. Pain, bewilderment and fear exploded about him until eventually it was too much for him to resist.

He went limp and when he no longer struggled

and hissed and mewed the children lost interest in him and ran off to play with something else.

They left him lying in the dust in a patch of sunlight, just outside the kitchen door. His silky, higgledy-piggledy coat was bedraggled and sticky. His eyes were shut.

The children's mother came out of the house and saw him lying there, looking quite dead. She pulled a wry face – she did not like animals – and decided to put him in the larder.

Her husband had brought the kitten home to catch a mouse. The smell of him alone would be enough to drive the intruder away and at least in the larder the children would not find him.

When Moshie Cat eventually recovered enough to grow aware of his surroundings, he found himself in a dark cool place which was decidedly pleasant. He found the courage to open his eyes, which were still blue and weak-looking, but saw nothing that he could recognize.

After a while he became aware of noises, children's voices, scampering feet, but they had forgotten him.

Twice the larder door was unexpectedly opened, flooding light into the darkness, and Moshie Cat fled behind some earthenware pots in a corner and hid there with madly pounding heart.

He stayed there on the second occasion, his black-and-white back pressed against the wall, his ears flicking in a cobweb that tickled. The soot on the pots smudged his snowy-white chest. He could have hidden inside one, he was so small.

The hours went by and Moshie Cat grew hungry. The house was silent now. The humans were in bed. The larder mouse began to make a noise and Moshie Cat pricked his ears. A cockroach waddled across the floor and he pounced on it.

He was in no mood to play, however, suddenly desolate in the dark larder which had grown quite cold and strange to him. He began to cry for his mother.

In a quiet, night-time house the cries of a lonely, hungry kitten are disturbing. They grow piercing and persistent. It seems that after a while they must stop, through sheer desperation on the part of the person awakened by them, but they do not.

They go on and on, louder still. The kitten cannot find its mother and has nothing to do but cry for her.

A light went on, shining through the netting that covered the larder door. Moshie Cat stopped crying, anticipating something.

It was the children's mother, bare-foot and in a nightdress that reached to her toes. She grabbed the kitten by the scruff, kept him dangling while she unlocked the front door, then threw him out into the darkness.

Moshie Cat landed against the wood pile and for a while was both silent and still, the breath crushed from his body. The smell of the olive wood was comforting and warm. He crept among the sawn branches and eventually fell asleep.

Moshie Cat runs away and hides in the geraniums

Moshie Cat was still asleep when the children came out of the house the next morning. They saw his white front paws peeping out from under a log and they soon had him out of his hiding place.

The three elder children had to go to school and they had no time to play more than cursorily with the kitten.

They splashed their faces with water which their mother had drawn up from the well and tipped into a plastic bowl; they tore at hunks of bread and chocolate, swallowed a glass of milk, and were off.

Moshie Cat was left in Tomasin's two-year-old hands. The little boy tried to pull out his black-and-white whiskers and seemed surprised when the kitten yowled.

The mother came and dragged the kitten from his grasp. She threw him into the corral with the hens to keep him away from the boy.

Still unresisting, Moshie Cat took no notice of the big white chickens that stalked up to him, wondering if he was good to eat. The boldest one, shaking her bright red comb, took a peck at him. She found the kitten not to her taste and wandered off.

A big buck rabbit came to sniff at him. The chicken came back and pecked at the rabbit for interfering with what was undoubtedly her property, she being mistress of the corral, and the rabbit fled.

Moshie Cat did not move from where the woman had flung him. Only a day before he had been round and sleek and playful. Now he was suddenly very thin-looking and bedraggled.

The sun grew high in the sky as the morning went by. It shone upon the tight green skins of pomegranates swelling slowly on the tree which hung over the corral. It shone down into the corral itself where the listless kitten lay. His black back began to glisten in the heat.

After a while he opened his eyes and twitched his ears. He was completely alone. The chickens and rabbits were hiding in the few shadows and had forgotten all about him.

He staggered to all fours and wandered jerkily about the corral. He began mewing for his mother, suddenly remembering her. He was ravenously hungry. No one had thought of giving him anything to eat.

He found a chunk of bread that the rabbits had not eaten. It was at least a week old and was as hard as stone. Gnawing at it only hurt his teeth. Saliva soaked his jaws but it did not soften the bread.

He chewed at a couple of feathers through which a breeze was whispering, their slight movement drawing his attention to them, but they only made him hungrier.

Eventually he also curled up in a shadow and fell asleep.

The children came again at lunchtime. They searched for Moshie Cat until they found him and dragged him from his sleep.

The girls dressed him again in their dolls' clothes, Rafael pushed him inside a biscuit box and banged on the sides. Then they went into lunch, called by their mother.

When they had gone Moshie Cat pushed his way out of the biscuit box. Trembling, terrified, he peered round its flaps then, seeing and hearing no one, he suddenly fled.

It seemed to Moshie Cat that he ran a long way. He came to a deserted, dusty lane and halted, pressed against the wall of a house. The lane spread out in three different directions, none of which would lead him back to his mother.

In the end he followed that which continued round the house. Dandelions and grass grew thickly against the old stone walls. They were cool and sheltering and quiet. A bee buzzed in one of the yellow flowers. It was the only sound and Moshie Cat, hearing it, was no longer so frightened. It was a sound he knew.

More slowly now he crawled through the grass and wild flowers until they came to an abrupt end against a huge, earthenware jar placed in their midst. Pink flowers hung down from the jar, touching the heads of the dandelions.

For a cautious length of time Moshie Cat

crouched unmoving. He was quite exhausted but fear drove him eventually on.

He had to traverse the open lane for quite a distance now – at least it seemed a long way to him, still small enough to sit in a person's hand – and his courage was failing.

The loud grunt of a nearby pig startled him into movement. He dashed out from his hiding place, shot along the lane, passed windows and doorways, and dived blindly into a jungle of red-and-white geraniums that decorated another house.

Moshie Cat did not know where he was, except that the flowers smelled friendly towards him. The earth was warm where they had their roots and their stems were so thick that he could hardly see between them.

The geranium bush made him believe that he was back in his own orchard, waiting for his mother to come and feed him, and so he stayed there, his back against a white wall and ignorant of the troop of ants that marched endlessly past him, occasionally dropping off into his hair.

He waited for hours and hours, sleeping sometimes. In the end his hunger was so agonizing and his loneliness so great that patience deserted him. He began to cry.

It brought him no result. The tortoiseshell cat did not come to him, nor did she hear him.

He cried intermittently for most of the afternoon, long hot hours, silent ones.

Moshie Cat finds a new home

Someone heard Moshie Cat crying. His wails sounded more like the cries of an injured nestling than a hungry kitten. They were so persistent, in spite of long lapses of silence, that the woman in the house felt obliged to look for the owner of them.

She went down to the orchard at the bottom of the garden and searched beneath the many almond trees there, whose leaves threw patterns across the dry soil, but no bird had fallen from its nest.

She searched among the piles of harvested beans, growing black and dry on the ground. She looked among the luxuriant growth of grass and thistles and dandelions that sprang up on the orchard's borders. She peered into the prickly pear tree where the tortoiseshell cat liked to laze.

Sometimes the sound seemed nearby; sometimes she lost it altogether. Sometimes she was certain that it was a bird, and then she would wonder if perhaps the sound was only imagined.

She set her children searching too, but the two small girls blundered about and made so much noise that they were not exactly helpful.

The sun was beginning to leave the sky when Moshie Cat was discovered among the roots of the geraniums that grew up to the living-room window.

His black-and-white face peered dolefully from beneath a furry green leaf and sheer chance caused the woman to see him.

Moshie Cat was afraid of people now. He hardly knew them but his short experience was enough to fill his small being with terror as hands came seeking into his hiding place, trying to grasp him.

He hissed and spat, his comical face suddenly tigerish, the dark eyes baleful. Tiny claws tore at the hands which sought to drag him from his refuge.

He crushed himself against the wall, causing havoc among the ant column, and clung desperately to each stalk and stem as he felt himself being dragged gradually into the open.

His body wriggled and his tail lashed as he was once again held in human grip, and he was too afraid to notice that the hands were strong but painless.

The only thing the woman noticed, apart from his savage fear, was the number of fleas that hurried hither and thither all over his white tummy.

She held him at arm's length, took him into the kitchen, found a cardboard box, and dropped him into it.

The children joggled curiously about him and Moshie Cat shrank. He pressed himself against the bottom of the box and snarled up at them silently. His eyes were narrow slits and he looked ferocious

enough, even in his smallness, to keep their eager hands at bay.

A saucer of bread and milk was placed in the box beside him but Moshie Cat was too afraid even to sniff at it. He only crushed himself farther into the corner he had found and forgot about being hungry.

Then a lid was put over the box and in its darkness Moshie Cat pondered. He did not touch the bread and milk, except to knock it over with his paws.

He crouched in the soggy mess and waited, muscles bunched, his senses confused by sounds and darkness, fear growing with every long minute that passed.

Not until the children were in bed did the mother

have time to think about the kitten. She returned to the captive, armed with insect powder, and lifted the lid.

It was all that Moshie Cat needed.

Like a black-and-white bullet he shot from the box and fled blindly across the kitchen, head down, searching refuge. Within a second he was underneath the refrigerator and there at least no one could reach him . . .

Not until two o'clock in the morning did Moshie Cat creep out of his hiding place. Moonlight lit up the silent kitchen, emphasizing the tallness of the tables and chairs, giants beside the kitten who was hardly more than a shadow on the faded red-and-orange tiles.

His cries woke up the woman and she came down the stairs in search of him. As the light went on, Moshie Cat shot under the refrigerator again. He still had no cause to trust anyone.

Twice more in the night the woman came down in answer to his cries and each time the kitten fled from her. There was no reaching him in his chosen hiding place and at last the woman left him to cry.

She came silently down the stairs again at seven o'clock, determined this time to catch him. Carefully she peered round the entrance.

Moshie Cat was almost at arm's length, his face twisted up as he tried to chew his way through a piece of bread that had escaped the broom the day before and which he had only just discovered.

He was completely unaware of the watcher until

28

suddenly he was in her grasp, too startled even to cry out.

His tail lashed, his head twisted wildly about, but this time there was no escape.

The woman warmed some milk, broke bread into it, and tipped the mixture into a saucer. She put a sheet of newspaper on the table, pulled up a chair, and placed Moshie Cat firmly in front of the saucer that rested on the newspaper.

The kitten struggled and dug his claws into the paper, pulling himself away from the saucer, but the woman would not let him go. She dipped a finger into the milk and rubbed it round the kitten's jaws and nose.

Moshie Cat snorted and struggled more but his tongue came out automatically to clean his milk-blocked nostrils. No sooner were they free when more milk was dabbed on to them.

Moshie Cat gave up the struggle. He licked his nose and grew quite excited. Soon he had his muzzle down to the plate, and he was lapping, lapping, noisy in his greed.

The hairs on his skinny frame stood up in excitement and bit by bit his tummy took on a bloated shape, accentuating the hollowness of the rest of him.

When the plate was clean he was returned, purring, to the cardboard box. An old rag was there for him to lie on and he began sucking at it avidly, all the while crooning, his claws digging in and out, in and out.

Soon he was asleep.

Explains how village cats
make themselves at home

It is very easy to collect cats if you live in a village where there are far too many of them and all of them hungry. The natives have their own ways of dealing with them.

True to a superstition that it is unlucky to kill an animal (except for meat) they prefer to drop them alive down the shaft of a dry well; take them out to the lonely hillsides and there abandon them, or even just leave them overnight on the main road where cars speed along at seventy or eighty miles an hour.

The cats in the neighbourhood of Moshie Cat's birthplace seemed to realize that the people who had just taken the end house in the lane were not natives. In next to no time the ever-flowering garden became their sanctuary.

Moshie Cat's mother almost lived in the prickly-pear tree, together with her one-eyed mate; a renegade tabby tom would survey the kitchen door from a shady spot beneath a yellow rose bush, hardly moving for hours; and another tabby, smaller, thinner, younger, would pass by from time to time.

Then there were Dracula, Fatty and Putchy, the

ones who became favourites for one reason or another, long before Moshie Cat arrived on the scene, and a white kitten that had stayed for a short while before dying.

On the very first day that the empty house was opened up, a black and exceedingly ferocious-looking cat strolled into the garden. The fact that he was not immediately attacked by broom or stones by the woman who moved about there gave him courage.

He sat on the gravel in the middle of the garden and stared at her. Soon he stretched a back leg into the air and started to lick it.

One ear was torn; the muzzle was scarred as is a railway terminus with tracks; and the eye-teeth were so long that they protruded from each side of his mouth, shining like vicious pearls in the brown-faded blackness of his jaw. He was so thin that he ought to have been dead.

He accepted a saucerful of milk unhurriedly, mulled over a plateful of rice and left it clean, then sat down again to wash himself.

His ablutions took up some fifteen minutes of his time before he was satisfied with the result. To the watching woman he looked no cleaner, just a bit damp in patches.

Then he stretched himself out in what remained of the evening sunlight and lay as if dead, except for the tip of his tail which twitched spasmodically from time to time at the chirp of a bird.

This was Dracula, who very soon condescended to enter the kitchen three or four times a week to eat up all the left-overs. He would wash himself in the kitchen, too, and even allow the two little girls to stroke him.

His brownness and his thinness began to fade.

A few days later another black cat joined him. She was also pitifully thin and had beautiful yellow eyes. She was very timid and would have fled at the sight of the woman had not Dracula shown her that there was nothing to be afraid of.

Dracula generously allowed her to share his left-overs and on most evenings their dark heads were bent over the same plate, their ears flicking rapidly whenever they accidentally touched and tickled.

When they had finished eating they would take up positions opposite each other, almost as if they were enemies, and start the paw-licking, ear-wiping, leg-biting and muzzle-rubbing routine which a meal always seems to encourage in a cat.

Then the she-cat would go away, called to other business, and sometimes Dracula would follow her. If she snarled at him he stayed behind, perfectly content.

Soon the she-cat lost her timidity and began to assert the authority of her sex. Dracula would re-treat from the plate until the other had eaten her fill, and she would leave him very litle.

It was she who now insidiously crept into the kitchen in search of comfort while Dracula be-haved like a gentleman and stayed outside.

This second cat, who had come like an empty paper bag, soon earned herself the name of Fatty.

She never stopped eating. She grew round and sleek and very contented. Her yellow eyes were moons of gentleness and so fond did she grow of the place where she was fed that she allowed the two little girls to do what they wanted with her, her paws soft and clawless in their presence.

She was a black pillow, to be found anywhere on the floor, on a chair, under the table, among the flowers. At night she had to be thrown out of the house, refusing to leave on invitation.

Mostly devoted to Putchy
although Fatty intervenes

Putchy was the only cat who really belonged to the family and who slept at night, by permission, on whichever bed he fancied most.

He had been brought to the house in a worse state than Moshie Cat, already resigned to death.

The woman had found him sitting among the rubbish that had been put out for the dustmen in the main street. He was about a month or six weeks old, a skeleton draped with stiff-haired skin, and he was as still as a discarded box or shoe, quite uninterested in his fate.

The woman took him home, unable to leave him there to be thrown away, still not dead.

When she put him to the floor he collapsed, but he was capable of gulping down the finely chopped liver she had bought for him in the butcher's shop. After this he was able to stagger to all fours and march stiffly marionette-fashion, out to the garden, where he proceeded to dig a deep hole, his boney front legs moving like shaky pistons.

Within a few days he was no longer quite so horrible to look at and the children even ventured to touch him, having recovered from their original distaste for him in his dust-ridden, cadaverous state.

He was a silver tabby with creamy throat and tiger's eyes. Gratitude or humility were never part of his nature. He was arrogant, savage without cause, and endlessly playful.

He was probably the most beautiful and well-cared-for cat in the village when Moshie came. The little girls were afraid of him and their father, who had an aversion to cats, was always saying, 'Why don't we throw him out?'

Fatty had prospered at Putchy's advent for, having taken the kitten under her wing, the woman felt she had to buy meat for him. She would cut it up into small chunks while Fatty looked on longingly, her yellow eyes unblinking.

At first the woman would throw her a scrap. Putchy had so much – he would sniff and study the bits of raw liver before deciding which to swallow first – and Fatty was always hungry, deserving of sympathy.

Fatty, of course, cleared up the kitten's left-overs, and then, bit by bit, she grew more artful. When Putchy was not looking she would stretch out a paw and draw small pieces away.

In the end it was necessary to feed her at the same time to keep her from stealing all Putchy's food. But she would gollop down her share at such a pace that she always finished first and still had time to steal from Putchy.

This went on until Putchy was bold enough to defend his rights. After that she did not dare steal openly from him.

Instead, she would draw close to him while he ate, cautiously place a paw over a piece of meat overlooked by its owner, and keep it there unmoving until Putchy had finished, licked his jaws and strolled away.

Only when he had gone, perhaps five minutes later, would Fatty pull the meat towards her and eat it. She was very patient.

Fatty grew fatter and fatter and fatter. She ate up all the chicken bones, all the left-overs, bits of bread and cake, as well as the small ration of fresh meat that she was given every day. She would also steal from the neighbours when the opportunity presented itself and catch mice and birds in the fields.

Often when Dracula came by there was nothing

left for him except perhaps a saucer of milk, of which he was particularly fond.

Putchy spent his kittenhood tearing Fatty's tail to pieces, pouncing all over her and learning to defend himself from her occasional annoyed reactions.

Sometimes she would hook a claw into the soft skin between his ears. That would keep him still for a long time, stretched out on the floor, afraid to move. Meanwhile Fatty dozed in peace, flicking the tip of her tail while Putchy watched with teased tiger eyes, unable to pounce.

In the middle of the summer Fatty had some kittens. She hid them away in a deserted barn nearby and the family in the end house saw little of her for a month or more.

She would come to eat, laze awhile among the roses, then return to her younglings. What eventually became of the litter can only be imagined. She returned to her patrons as fat as ever and brought no offspring with her.

She took to climbing the pomegranate tree in the orchard and showed Putchy how it was done. Soon the two of them were racing up and down all the trees available to them, Fatty stretched out on the high branches like an indolent black panther, Putchy clinging to the lower ones, whipping his striped tail back and forth.

They passed a delightful summer together and washed each other's heads and throats, purring rhythmically.

All this poor Dracula saw with envy. He hated

Putchy, looking upon him as a possible future rival, but was too much the gentleman to do him any harm. He contented himself with hissing so fiercely that Putchy would fling himself up the stairs and take refuge under a bed, stricken with terror.

Dracula would hiss all round the kitchen, his long teeth gleaming, grab whatever was thrown down for him and dash out of the house, loping with his prize to the bottom of the orchard.

From there he slipped under the barbed wire fencing to the dried-up torrent, where he could chew over his morsel unseen and unmolested, crouched among withered branches from the last winter's rains.

When the nights at last grew cold Fatty refused to be turned out of the house. She would hide in the fireplace in the kitchen until she was either forgotten or until the woman believed she had already gone.

By the time her tricks were discovered, the people's hearts were softened towards her and she was allowed to stay, which had been her intention in the first place.

She and Putchy slept together on the warm bricks, creeping right over the slumbering ashes during the night. By the end of the winter black Fatty had grown quite grey.

She repaid the humans with such trust that one wet April morning, when the garden was drowned in puddles and the barley in the orchard was beaten down, she produced another litter of kittens on a cushion in the fireplace.

She looked so proud of her family, purring deeply, and was certain that no one would harm them, that the woman was blackmailed into accepting them.

So it was that when Moshie Cat joined the family, the house was already full of kittens that the woman did not know what to do with.

In which Moshie Cat is kidnapped

By nine o'clock that morning Moshie Cat had been revived by sleep and was outside again, exploring the new home he had found for himself.

Dew still clung to the plants in the shadows and the earth under the ivy was damp and black. He decided that it was still too cold for him there.

He lamb-skipped back to the rose tree beside the kitchen door and began patting the fallen red petals tentatively, his paws as velvet as they were.

He discovered his tail and began chasing it furiously, round and round and round again. Then he dropped down abruptly in the middle of his whirls to bite at a hind leg which was tickling him.

At this moment Fatty returned. She had gone off early in the morning on wanderings of her own and obviously had still not discovered the existence of Moshie Cat in the house, or else had forgotten, for she came loping into the garden with an anxious cry, thinking that the black-and-white kitten was one of her own.

Moshie Cat jumped up with an answering mew. At the same time Fatty realized her mistake. She was close to him now and Moshie was beginning to purr, thinking he had found himself a new mother.

He wriggled up to her, rubbing his head against her soft black flank.

She drew back with a hiss as if suddenly stabbed. The hair on her back went stiff, and her tail was like a thick wire brush as she slashed out with her claws.

Moshie Cat, too, was suddenly frozen into spikes. He cringed and snarled and flattened himself to the gravel.

Fatty's yellow eyes outstared him. He suddenly turned tail and dashed for the safety of the geranium bush. It shook for a few seconds, then was still.

Fatty's hair resumed its silky softness and she strolled into the kitchen as if nothing had perturbed her. She slid through the bead curtains of the larder under the stairs, where her family was hidden, and by the sounds that shortly came from that direction it could be assumed that it was being fed.

Moshie Cat's black nose peered out from under a leaf. The garden was deserted except for a blue-tit perched on the white rose bush.

He wriggled out from his hiding place and, in a second, was prancing and twisting and skipping again, his fright forgotten. The tit, with a flick of its wings, swooped away.

Moshie Cat spent the whole morning playing with leaves and stones and flowers. The children raced about the garden with a long string to which was attached a screw of newspaper.

The kitten was tireless in pursuit of it and even Fatty deigned to tap at it with a curious paw now and then. She had decided for the moment at least that the newcomer was harmless.

At midday Rafael, Mari-Loli, Manolita and Tomasin came looking for their kitten. Their house backed on to the house in which Moshie Cat had at last found refuge and it was only a matter of time before he was discovered.

Elenita flung herself into the kitchen, screaming and in tears. 'Mama, Rafael has taken the kitten. He's gone back to his house with it.'

The woman dropped everything and dashed round to the neighbour's house, her daughters anxiously behind. They discovered the children grouped round their doorway, the kitten at their feet, motionless and cowed.

'It's my kitten,' stated Rafael, righteously indignant.

'I found it in my garden, almost dying of hunger. You should look after it better if it's your kitten.'

'It got lost.'

Rafael's mother appeared in the doorway. She greeted her neighbour with a smile, smoothing the hair away from her forehead.

'What's the matter? Oh, is that kitten back again!'

'That's what I've come about,' and the woman explained again how she had found it in the garden.

'You can keep it if you want it. I don't like animals in the house.'

Rafael began to howl. 'But it's my kitten. Papa brought it home for me.'

'He can always get you another. Give it to the lady.'

Rafael hung back. He had the kitten in his arms now, crushed against his breast. Perhaps in his way he loved it.

'I'll buy it from you,' suggested the neighbour, watched silently by all the children, their big brown eyes the only attractive part of their pinched faces.

'No! He'll give it to you, won't you, Rafael? Papa will get you another. A white one, much prettier. You'll see.'

Reluctantly, sulkily, Rafael dropped the kitten in the woman's outstretched hands. Moshie Cat dug in his claws, still frightened. But he relaxed slowly as the woman scratched at his throat with her thumb. Soon he was purring.

Moshie Cat is rejected by
his mother and meets Putchy

It was a day of surprises and adventures for Moshie
Cat. That evening he was playing about in what
was left of the day's sunshine, trying to catch his tail
in a surprise attack, when the Tortoiseshell came
tentatively up to the kitchen door.

She would do this only rarely for she was always
timid. The woman had tried to encourage her with
scraps of food. She was undoubtedly the prettiest
cat in the neighbourhood, with eyes as orange as
the patches on her flanks.

But she was as shy as the wild birds and only
great hunger would tempt her to the door.

There was a chicken claw which the woman had
kept for three days in the event that Dracula might
turn up. He had not come round for a week. She
would give it to the Tortoiseshell as a reward for
having found the courage to come so close. It would
be a pity to disappoint her.

Even as the cat stood quiveringly near the doorstep, ready for flight, Moshie saw her and suddenly
realized who she was.

His black tail went straight up and he ran at full
speed to his mother, yowling his delight.

But the mother cat spat at him. She no longer

recognized her higgledy-piggledy son. Kittenless once again, she had forgotten that so short a time ago she had been a mother.

Now she was just an independent she-cat, selfish to all except her own desires. She dozed all day in the prickly-pear tree or hunted in the fields and torrent with her one-eyed shadow.

Moshie Cat could not accept her rejection of him. He fawned about her, piebald body wriggling, his back on the ground, his forepaws stretched out at her. And all the while he mewed like a baby, pleading with her.

The Tortoiseshell huffed herself up and jumped

away. Under the yellow-flowering honeysuckle, where the shadows were dark and the mosquitoes hung in clouds, the one-eyed cat was waiting for her.

She fled back to him, as if afraid of the kitten, and Moshie Cat rolled to all fours, staring after her but not daring to follow.

For a minute the two animals stood beside the rambling honeysuckle, ears flicking at the hungry mosquitoes.

The woman threw the chicken claw in their direction and they fled, disappearing along the cat-paths of the prickly-pear tree into the gathering darkness.

Moshie Cat bounded after the claw and brought it back to the kitchen. He tortured it for a while, imagining perhaps that it was a mouse. He was stretched out on one flank and never let it escape his paws. His cockeyed face had the expression of a clown.

It must have been past ten o'clock that night when Putchy pushed his striped head against the door to open it and strolled into the kitchen. He had been away from home for three days and returned as nonchalantly as ever.

He threw himself down on the tiles, effortless in all his movements. One never saw him do anything until it was done. But in a moment he was on all fours again, yellow eyes narrowed, ears pricked.

He had discovered Moshie Cat, who was nodding beneath the table with his paws tucked under him, almost asleep.

Putchy stalked all about the table, curious, excited. Moshie Cat opened his eyes and watched him, afraid to move.

Then Putchy sat down in front of him and stared.

Moshie Cat still did nothing, not even move a whisker. They watched each other motionlessly.

Putchy wanted to play. He stretched out suddenly on his flank and tapped at Moshie Cat with a paw.

The kitten drew into himself a little more without actually moving from the spot. His eyes were on Putchy's wagging tail-tip. Suddenly he pounced!

It was a mistake he was to commit time and time again. In the same instant the big tabby's body was curled about him and the kitten was helpless in his grasp. Cruel back claws raked him and at the same time his ears and neck were chewed.

The woman swiped at Putchy with a dish-cloth and they were parted, Moshie Cat to fly to his refuge under the fridge, the lord of the house to sit and lick his creamy chest, unperturbed.

Putchy's tail-tip was still wagging and Moshie Cat was watching it from his hiding place.

He darted out, unable to resist temptation, skidded on the silky tail and fled back, all in a second. Putchy was behind him, grabbing with his claws, but he was too big to get under the fridge and Moshie Cat was safe.

They carried on in this fashion for some ten minutes or so until in the end Putchy had caught

Moshie Cat at least three times and thoroughly punished him.

The last tussle dragged howls out of the kitten and when at last he escaped, saved by the dish-cloth again, he was too subdued to desert his hiding place.

Putchy gave up waiting for him after a while, especially when Moshie Cat was not even tempted by the paw he pushed under the fridge, and he went up to bed.

Fatty had watched this display with bored interest, sitting beside the larder under the stairs.

When everything was quiet, with Putchy upstairs and Moshie Cat decidedly under the fridge, she slipped in to her kittens and nestled down in the old log basket beside them, purring, purring.

In which Moshie Cat
nearly strangles himself

The geraniums which had first sheltered Moshie Cat when he ventured into the garden of the end house became his favourite playground.

Their lower stems were thick and trunk-like while the upper ones were top-heavy with pink and white blooms and a myriad of leaves. They were tied back to the wall to prevent the stems from snapping and were thus reasonably secure against Moshie Cat's first attempts at climbing.

This great bush was, to him, a jungle tree. He wriggled and twisted along the stems, nestling in the joints to tap at his dangling tail or to examine gingerly a strange insect that happened to be sharing the same road.

The flowers staggered under his restless weight. Blossoms were scattered by his mischievous claws and leaves were shredded.

But worse damage still was inflicted when Moshie Cat suddenly lost his balance and crashed to the ground, bringing with him all that his claws had grabbed at in vain.

One afternoon Moshie Cat found a piece of string that dangled from the wall beside the geraniums. After a first tentative examination told him that it was harmless, he pounced on it, ears flattened, tail whipping.

He reared on to his hind legs and held it between his front paws, biting at it with distasteful expression.

He patted it, he purred over it. It was his friend. It was his enemy. He went quite mad over it with joy and rage.

Only Fatty noticed what he was doing. She was sitting on the kitchen doorstep, dozing in the sunshine, and now and again she gazed sleepily in his direction, faintly interested in his furious, silent game.

The children were splashing about with two buckets of water and the woman was weeding in another part of the garden.

Moshie Cat had reached the conclusion that the string was an inert and lifeless object, not half as much fun as the one the humans had teased him with earlier, with its bits of rustling paper.

He was frightened when he discovered that in some subtle manner it had fastened itself about his body.

He sprang up and began to struggle, and then the string came to life with a vengeance, embedding itself deeper into him with every movement, winding itself about his neck.

Fatty opened her eyes a little wider and pricked her ears. She wondered what Moshie Cat was up to and had some sense of his fear.

He was fighting desperately now, clawing at his throat, trying to tear at the string which had him half-suspended from the ground. He could not even cry out, his open mouth choked by his tongue.

For a second he stopped fighting, but panic surged through him as the string tightened still more, cutting off his breath.

His baby-blue eyes bulged, his lungs burned. The only sound he could utter was a faint hiss which was scraped from the very depths of despair.

He struggled some more, but feebly, for already the light had gone out of his day and darkness was all about him.

Fatty was watching intently now, sleep forgotten. She saw the woman suddenly spring to her feet, at last aware of the kitten's predicament.

But to Moshie Cat, crazed with imminent strangulation, the hands that took hold of him and began rapidly to unwind the string were enemies too.

Twice he sunk all his teeth into the woman's hand, causing her to drop him so that he was jerked still more fiercely, but at last he fell free from the string and fled.

He hid in the shadowy coolness of the creeping ivy that grew against the wall of the next-door neighbour's pigsty. Sunk into the soft soil, he panted and shook until his lungs were no longer tortured and his fear had gone.

He stayed there until darkness came. The garden was empty except for the bats that flew jerkily from the eaves of the house, and the huge moths that came to drink the scents from the night-time flowers.

The lantern above the kitchen door suddenly sprang into brightness and Moshie Cat pricked his ears.

Fatty strolled out of the house and sat in the centre of a pool of light on the gravel, licking herself, and Putchy suddenly ran out also, tail high. He loped off on business of his own after a quick pounce on Fatty, which bowled her over and startled her.

Moshie Cat watched the half-open kitchen door for a long time. It was not far away, but he was still afraid. Did the clinging monster still lie in wait for him beside the geraniums?

At last hunger and the need for comfort overcame fear. He pulled in his muscles, hesitated a second longer, quivering with the need for courage, then in one mad dash reached the door and streaked into the kitchen.

There was milk and raw meat waiting for him, which it pained him to swallow, but afterwards he was purring on the woman's lap while her fingers rubbed between his ears.

There was no greater paradise than this.

Moshie Cat discovers the world upstairs and is thrown out of a window

Putchy decided that Moshie Cat was his plaything. He suddenly stopped wandering off on his own. Instead he hunted down Moshie Cat and took charge of him, introducing him to the upstairs world of which the kitten had been quite ignorant. Moshie Cat was picked up by the scruff of the neck and carried, unprotesting, up the stairs to Putchy's favourite room.

This was a kind of combined study and sitting-room of huge dimensions. Moshie Cat, plumped down in the middle of the beige, imitation marble tiles, felt quite lost there.

In one corner was a fireplace surrounded by books and small pictures; two walls were taken up by gigantic chests of drawers and numerous chairs; near the door were more shelves full of books and not far from the fireplace, in front of a French window which gave on to a tiny balcony, was a black wooden desk.

In front of the fireplace were two chairs. One was almost big enough for a giant to sit in, made of thick wood, studded with brass nails and covered with red velvet. The other was very small, with a raffia seat. Both of them were Putchy's.

But the tabby's favourite place was the balcony, where he would sit for hours when he was at home. From there he had a wonderful view over the garden.

With pricked ears and quivering body, his tail-tip flicking to and fro, he would watch all the cats that strayed past the door, and could even see the sheep grazing in the meadow on the other side of the torrent.

When he was in a hurry to leave the house, he would spring from the balcony to the grape-vine, which grew in a sheltered buttress nearby, and run down its trunk to the ground.

The balcony and all the window were surrounded by the red roses which grew up from beside the kitchen door, just beneath.

Before Moshie Cat could finish his surveillance of the room, looking for a suitable retreat and intimidated by the size of everything, Putchy grabbed him again.

He padded about the room like a tiger with a rabbit between its jaws and jumped up on the desk. Pinning Moshie Cat under his paw with unsheathed claws, he began licking him all over.

Moshie Cat purred at first but then Putchy began biting and the purrs changed to yowls of pain.

Putchy allowed the kitten to escape, falling off the desk in his haste. He galloped across the polished tiles towards the inviting darkness underneath one of the chests of drawers, skidded, fell flat on his tummy and almost knocked himself out.

He felt the big cat pounce on him again and was carried this time to the huge red chair, his head between the other's jaws. A second time Putchy relentlessly set about washing, stroking and biting him and Moshie Cat alternately purred and cried.

When Putchy relaxed his grip, Moshie Cat escaped, leaping from the chair and this time reaching the safety of one of the chests, whose foot was as small and as round as he was.

But the sight of Putchy's madly lashing tail, and the tabby paws that patted at him were irresistible. They drew him out like the hook in a fish's mouth.

He was too eager to play and too forgetful of Putchy's fierce nature to stay hidden for long and from then on he spent the best part of his waking hours flying from the big tabby, who drew howls out of him each time he caught him.

Moshie Cat almost forgot that the garden existed, engrossed by this strange world of furniture that smelled of polish, and the shining floor in which his image was vaguely reflected.

He even ventured on to Putchy's tiny balcony when the big cat was not there and jumped on the butterflies that had come to rest in the sunshine.

The bees that buzzed in the hearts of the roses also fascinated him. Their sound, their movement was enough to drive any playful kitten into a frenzy, but he had not the courage to venture into the branches of the rose tree, for the ground was a long way away.

He discovered a small window which had been let into the wall. Below it was a tiled seat with a striped cushion. It was a low seat, into which Moshie Cat could struggle with a certain amount of effort, and as there did not seem to be any smell of Putchy about it, he took it for his own.

From then on he would sleep nowhere else at night. Putchy would carry him upstairs in his mouth, sometimes knocking the limp body against the stairs, and the woman would carry him down before going to bed, dropping him firmly into his box.

As soon as the lights were out Moshie Cat was out of the box and dragging himself up the stairs again.

The moon-filled room had frightened him at first, its weird light making strange shapes of the daylight world, but the smells were the same so he took heart.

He would swing himself up on the cushion, making holes in it with his claws, and the very silence of the house would lull him into slumber.

Night insects sometimes banged against the window-panes, but he did not hear them. He slept always on his back, his legs tucked into his tummy, his head dangling right off the cushion. Sometimes he lost balance and woke up with a start on the floor.

He would sleep until the moon had gone and the sun had come again, until Fatty was scratching at the kitchen door and miauing to be let out, and he would half-turn, half-slide, half-tumble down the stairs to join her.

One morning, very early, when Fatty still dozed with her kittens in the downstairs larder, when Putchy still had not returned from his nocturnal huntings, Moshie Cat was woken in a different manner. Someone was stroking him.

It was the younger of the two little girls. Moshie Cat, still half asleep, stretched luxuriantly, his throat already humming with pleasure. He was no longer frightened of the humans. In this house no one had ever hurt him.

The little girl, who was only two, lifted the catch and opened the window. She picked up Moshie Cat, still purring and digging his claws into the striped cushion, and tossed him out. Then she shut the window, padded back to bed, and fell asleep.

A week of surprises

It was altogether a troublesome week for Moshie Cat. For the first three days of it he could hardly walk, his back bruised and one of his haunches swollen.

He clung to the quiet corners of the house where no one would molest him. Even Putchy seemed to recognize that he was not well and left him alone. He would eat nothing, a fact that Fatty quickly took advantage of, cleaning his plate before it could be retrieved.

He had no understanding of why he had been thrown out of the window and did not even know what had caused him to go suddenly sailing through the air, to land with a thud on the sharp gravel of the garden path.

He demonstrated no fear of anyone but just wanted to be left alone.

But after three days he was suddenly prancing and dashing about again, eating with ravenous hunger to make up for his long fast, daring to attack Putchy's tail. He was still a bit lame but even the limp eventually disappeared, unnoticed by anyone.

He dragged himself upstairs again and returned to sleeping on his favourite cushion. The sad, withdrawn face was comical and eager again and the little paws never still.

Moshie Cat discovered that the big upstairs room was no longer the same. All the books had been pulled down from the shelves and a few of them rested on the red chair.

Putchy sent these flying three or four times until the woman chased him out of the house, and Moshie Cat crouched between the chair legs, tapping cautiously at a few sheets of paper that were scattered there.

He clambered in and out of packing-cases, after examining them for unfriendly smells and finding none. Sometimes he could get in but not get out, and eventually he fell asleep among the books at the end of the day, so warm and inviting were they.

That night the room looked like nothing he had previously known. The moon shone only fitfully from a troubled sky and the floor was a mass of weird shadows and papers that rustled in a draught that crept under the door.

There was a mumble of distant thunder and every now and then a brilliant flash of light savagely contorted the different shapes.

Moshie Cat hardly dared lift his black-and-white head from the books where he had buried it. Even the air was different that night and the wind that bustled about was a hot one.

Unexpectedly, the menacing stillness was sundered by a crack of thunder that seemed to split the world itself. Simultaneously, a torrent of rain gushed over the rooftops and the noise of it, like a million poundings overhead, almost frightened Moshie Cat more than the thunder.

He shot out of the crate as if the lightning that had been playing over the floor and windows for half the night had suddenly attacked him personally, and he fled to his favourite place of safety beneath the century-old chest of drawers.

While thunder whipped over the house and the rain threatened to break the window-panes with its force, Moshie Cat crouched and trembled behind the chest's round foot.

His dark blue eyes stared fearfully at the light that flickered all over the broken sky, and the scattered books were sinister in the alternate dark and light. Not far from where he hid there was a steady patter of water dripping to the floor.

When the storm passed Moshie Cat ventured out again. The sky was tossed but the moon shone clearly. Lightning still flickered occasionally but it no longer frightened him.

He climbed back into the box of books and, purring like an engine, fell asleep.

The next day the garden was a place of electric enchantment, every plant bristling with new smells and sensations.

Snails meandered everywhere, among the roses, the ivy, the grape-vines. They climbed up the kitchen door and stuck to the toys the children had left out overnight.

But in the house Fatty was mewing plaintively, anxiously watching the transfer of her kittens from the log basket to a paper-lined box, and not under-standing the reason for it.

The box with its three surprised occupants was carried to an outhouse not far away, belonging to a neighbour who already knew the black she-cat well, and Fatty was not seen for most of that day. She worried over her kittens and the new home and hardly dared to leave them.

At supper-time she came back for something to eat. Afterwards she stopped in the middle of the kitchen floor to wash herself and, having glanced once into the larder to make sure that her young-lings really had been removed, waddled off along the garden path to her new home.

Perhaps she had already suspected that one day this would happen. She had never found herself an owner for such a long time before.

The following afternoon it took at least an hour of struggles and scratches, wild howls, snarls and tigerish leaps to get Putchy into the box that was to transport him to his new home.

When at last he was firmly imprisoned, the box shook and rattled with the fury it contained. It was placed gingerly in the boot of the car. No one dared travel with it.

Everything was ominously quiet now. Had he died of suffocation or was he preparing himself for a final attack which would smash the box to pieces with his thunderball tactics?

Moshie Cat sat on his mistress' lap inside the car. He was considered too small to be troublesome and, apart from digging his claws fiercely into the woman's legs and making fitful attempts to escape every now and then, he was fairly calm about his first car journey.

He was more curious than worried about the new house, too, and sat on the window-ledge of the bedroom in which he had been locked, looking at the unusual scenery with pricked ears.

It was mostly bricks and cement as the window looked out on to a gigantic water tank. A sparrow pecked along a jutting-out ledge of the tank, unaware of its keen-eyed watcher.

Putchy's box had been set down on the floor in the middle of an empty room almost fearfully. Windows and door were shut, children were banned. The strings and wires were carefully withdrawn and the lid opened with the greatest delicacy.

The lord of the house strolled out of his confinement as if he had passed a most agreeable half-hour there and proceeded at once to lick his ruffled fur.

Dogs and workmen and
the sound of strange cats

Moshie Cat's fourth home was different from the third in that it had no upstairs. It was a bungalow-type chalet and the only steps were outside the house where he was afraid to venture.

There was no garden in this new place, only a big paved yard with a few pine trees of various sizes where dozens of sparrows nested.

The yard gave directly on to a road, along which little traffic passed except the huge lorries that came five or six times a day with water for the tank. Rising steeply up from this was a thick pine wood, its chalky ground bare except for the heather and gorse that stuck up stiffly everywhere.

The summer air vibrated with the sound of crickets, night and day, and at dusk the sparrows settled noisily into their nests, wheeling and squabbling until a general accord was reached when, apart from a few cheeps, they were suddenly silent.

On either side of Moshie Cat's new home were neighbours. On one side, beyond the water tank, they were too far away to make their presence known. On the other side, with not even a fence to separate them from his own yard, were two small dwellings. In one lived a huge Alsatian, in the other a small wire-haired fox terrier.

Putchy discovered the existence of the Alsatian on his first morning in the new home. He had ventured out of doors but, before he could even begin to scratch a hole in the sand that surrounded one of the pine trees, a great black-and-tan animal was towering over him, terrible sounds issuing from its hot, open mouth.

Putchy had never seen a dog before, but instinct and courage told him how to behave. Every hair on his body stuck out like the quills of a hedgehog until he seemed twice as large as before. His face contorted into fury, his claws as far-stretched as they would go.

He swelled himself up from the ground, not an eighth of the dog's size, but intimidating enough to keep her at bay.

Around and around him the dog worried, whining, growling, plumy tail waving excitedly. And Putchy kept a hypnotic gaze into the dog's eyes, daring her to close in, hissing savagely.

The incident was brought to an abrupt close by the arrival of both Putchy's mistress and the dog's. The dog was chased back to her house and the moment Putchy found himself out of danger he fled across the road in a couple of bounds, leapt up the bank through which the road had been cut and was lost among the bracken of the pine wood.

He did not return till nightfall.

Meanwhile Moshie Cat had discovered a terror

of his own and it was something that was to haunt him always.

Directly behind the house was a hotel to which a number of additions were in the process of being completed. Part of the yard belonging to Moshie Cat's home had been commandeered by the labourers working there, together with their bricks and cement and tools.

The workmen had to cross the yard to the well to fetch water. They wore big boots or cement-caked sandals. They pushed wheelbarrows, clanged about with pipes, and altogether made a great disturbance.

They also believed that cats only existed for their amusement.

They laughed when the tiny Moshie Cat ventured out into the yard with his timid gait and funny black nose. One of them stamped a foot right behind him and he fled back to the kitchen, terrified.

When he gathered the courage to go out again the same process was repeated until he lost his nerve and stayed trembling in an obscure corner. The workmen found it very funny.

In the following days and weeks and months these men were Moshie Cat's purgatory. The noise they made with their spades and buckets and boots; their constant movements, back and forth, up and down the steps that led to the hotel and passed right beside the kitchen door, drove him into a state of constant panic.

Once one of the workmen grabbed him as he tried to cross the yard and threw him right into the face of the Alsatian who happened to be there at the same time.

The dog was as startled as the kitten was terrified and Moshie Cat had scrabbled panic-stricken back to the kitchen by the time the Alsatian came slavering in his wake.

From then on Moshie Cat refused to move out of the house while the workmen were about and became frightened of every loud sound or unexpected movement. His only relief from fear came in the evening when at last they had gone away and on Sundays when they did not work.

Then he would consent to explore in the yard, smell at the pine bark and sit and wash himself or chase his tail.

Foreign tourists passing along the road would stop and watch him. He was still very tiny and comical to look at. But if they snapped their fingers or called to him he would fly into the kitchen again and find a dark corner to hide in.

Putchy superciliously ignored the workmen. Every morning he would disappear into the pine woods and rarely return before nightfall, and often not even then. He preferred to prowl about outside.

The silent nights were sometimes broken by a rising crescendo of howls and growls. The listening Moshie Cat would tremble and run to the kitchen door, but during the first weeks at least no strange cats were ever seen during the daytime.

Now that Putchy preferred to spend most of his nights out of doors, Moshie Cat took over the vacated space on the humans' bed.

He learned after a number of fruitless adventures to higher regions that the correct position was at the woman's feet. If he stayed right there no one would disturb him. If he ventured over to the man's side one hard push would shoot him on to the floor, so he did not make that mistake very often.

He purred himself into slumber, digging his claws into the counterpane, and hardly stirred the whole night long unless a shriek from a maundering cat startled him into wakefulness.

He spent the best part of the day curled up on a chair in the kitchen and, unlike Putchy, he became a very homey sort of cat, gentle, unobtrusive, but terribly, terribly clumsy.

The hunting of sparrows
and other things

Cats generally are noted for their agility, their sure-footedness, their split-second timing and accurate judgement when scaling heights, narrow ledges, swaying branches or even chair-backs.

Moshie Cat was different.

For no explicable reason he would decide to jump up on the table when everyone was having lunch. More than once he landed in the middle of someone's plate, scattering both dish and meal over wall and floor.

He would only spring from floor to chair, or from bed to floor, when someone was passing by, causing a confused collision which was startling if painless.

Good at climbing trees, the prospect of coming down terrified him. This perhaps is not so unusual in cats, but Moshie Cat would never allow himself to be rescued, even by his mistress, without working himself up into a state of nervous dithers.

After half an hour of calling and coaxing, with outstretched hands willing to grasp him, he would take a flying leap, usually directly into the woman's face.

If nothing could persuade him to attempt the

downward journey – and it sometimes happened that he spent half a day gripping fearfully to the branch of a pine tree – he would have to be dragged down ignominiously by a leg or his tail.

Moshie Cat was always getting fish and chicken bones stuck between his teeth, something that Putchy and Fatty and Dracula never did. And he would frequently get himself locked inside cupboards and wardrobes.

He loved to sit in the bathroom, under the shower (at least he had the sense to sit there only when it was turned off) but directly from the shower he would jump up on one of the beds with wet paws and tail.

One of Moshie Cat's favourite pastimes, once the workmen had gone, was hunting birds. There were so many sparrows twittering about the yard that it should have been an easy business. But Moshie Cat was as clumsy in his hunting as in everything.

He would stroll out of doors, stop with a jerk at the sight of a congregation of small squabblers a few feet away, then without a moment's planning or forethought pounce among them.

Of course they always got away. They were on the wing at his first pounce. He would swirl about the now vacant spot with lashing tail and sparkling eyes, and the sparrows would scold him from the safety of a high branch in the pine tree.

As the time went by and all his efforts were frustrated, Moshie Cat learned to be more cautious.

He would creep snake-fashion towards the tree, hide behind the trunk and watch the sparrows, his black-and-white form completely immobile but for the quivering tail-tip.

But the very effort of so much concentration was too much for him. He was hypnotized by his rigidity, and the birds usually startled him into a backward spring as of one accord they abruptly flew away, still unaware of his presence.

Moshie Cat was determined to catch himself a sparrow and one day he actually succeeded.

The whole summer had gone by in futile effort and it was in the gloom of a November morning that he slunk into the house with a bird between his jaws.

His whole gait was altered. The kitten in him was suddenly lost. He was a hunter, with the taste of warm blood on his tongue.

His gentle eyes narrowed and sharp, his ears flattened against his skull, he kept to the shelter of the walls as he slunk round the kitchen and made for the children's bedroom, where he supposed he could devour his prize in seclusion.

The sparrow was still alive, jerking a wing, fluttering, and the children cried out the news and chased after him.

Moshie Cat fled for the bedroom, the whole family in pursuit. He was dragged unwillingly from under a bed, growling as he had never done in his whole short lifetime.

He was determined not to let the bird go. It had taken him six months to capture it.

'Leave him alone,' said the man to his wife. 'He might bite you.'

But the woman had held Moshie Cat too often in her arms and had spent too many evenings stroking him, while he purred in harmony, to distrust him now.

Moshie Cat growled and wriggled and clenched the sparrow tighter. The bird flapped spasmodically. The woman pressed her fingers firmly into the cat's jaws until slowly his mouth was forced open and the sparrow fell into her hand.

Too gentle with his prize, Moshie Cat had not hurt the sparrow unduly. There was a spot of blood under one eye but that was all and it flew away towards the sea, none the worse for its adventure.

Moshie Cat prowled about the place where the woman had released it, his tail still lashing.

After a while he returned to his favourite hiding place behind the pine tree and prepared himself to wait for another opportunity. But he never did catch another bird.

Astor and Moshie Cat
reach an agreement

It was rather strange that Moshie Cat, who was so afraid of the workmen that timidity became a part of his character, should, after a first rather stiff and unfriendly introduction, get on to quite tolerable terms with the next-door fox terrier.

Astor was a dog old enough to have developed quite a character. She was fussy and spoiled, a lady in her manners, but true to her terrier blood she could not abide cats.

If there were no stray cats in the neighbourhood it was because Astor always kept them well at bay.

She would chase an unsuspecting cat halfway down the road, barking frantically, blood boiling with excitement, or hold a tree'd cat at bay for the whole of an afternoon.

Putchy and Moshie Cat were quite a problem for, of course, she immediately understood that they belonged to a friend of her mistress and were therefore untouchable.

When she felt that she could get away with it, she would chase after them in high spirits. But such an escapade would get her locked up for hours, and a scolding into the bargain, so she decided it was best to ignore them.

Putchy was easily ignored, and best left alone. Even the big Alsatian was wary now of starting up Putchy. The proud creature would fly straight at the dog's face without any provocation, and in fact it was necessary to protect the Alsatian from the cat.

Moshie Cat was a different proposition. He was only a kitten, harmless in his way. Astor soon grew into the habit of spending her many lonely hours with the new neighbour and the kitchen was usually occupied by Moshie Cat.

Astor would drink the kitten's milk and gobble up any left-overs on his plate. She would stick up her nose and sniff at Moshie Cat's feet, where he crouched all stiff on a chair, causing him to spring up in alarm. But this was only the natural greeting between cat and dog.

Soon Moshie Cat would lie in wait for the dog, one leg dangling idly down from the chair. As Astor passed by, he would tap out teasingly, causing the dog to start.

Astor longed to be revenged, but she knew that it was not polite and so restrained herself.

In the summer evenings Moshie Cat's mistress visited at the fox-terrier's house. Moshie Cat found himself lonely.

He wandered along to the neighbour, slunk up the steps to her terrace, and Astor gave the alarm, whimpering wildly at the gate.

Moshie Cat, knowing that the dog could not reach him, sat a breath's pace away, his back disdainfully turned towards Astor while he set about washing his ears and tail.

Astor whined and moaned and gasped with frustration, the cat so near and yet untouchable, and Moshie Cat poked his paws between the bars, pulling at the terrier's woolly legs when he could.

By winter Astor and Moshie Cat shared the same sofa. They grumbled all the while at each other, dozing uneasily, but both were too comfortable to move.

There was but one extra cat that nosed about the yard. This was a lean, miserable-looking tabby who lived at a boarding-house not far away. He was a hanger-on who was prepared to go to any lengths and suffer any indignity for a bit of comfort or a mouthful of food.

He fawned round every passer-by, effusively affectionate, and would long ago have crept into the woman's kitchen had not Putchy still been master there.

Both Putchy and Astor hated him. Putchy persecuted him nearly every night, his growls and the other's piercing, terrified screams echoing in the starlight.

Astor vented her frustration and fury on him and, although she was not a vicious dog, she would have joyfully torn a chunk out of him.

In spite of this Stripes, as he was eventually called, persisted in hanging about, waiting for the bits and pieces that would be flung to him by the woman, who still could not accustom herself to the idea that, in that part of the world at least, hunger was a cat's natural state.

Moshie Cat's winter friend

That winter Moshie Cat found a friend.

He was a well-grown kitten now, getting on for nine months old, almost a cat. His body was plump, his eyes were big and yellow and innocent-looking, and sometimes Putchy ran away from him.

The two creatures plundered beds, sprang across tables, and performed gymnastics on the chairs with wagging tails and outstretched claws.

But Putchy was less and less often at home, the pine woods across the road claiming his wild spirit.

If Moshie Cat missed him it was only because he was bored on his own. Of Stripes and the other tom-cats that wandered about, he was still young enough to be frightened, and he spent the best part of the day sleeping in the kitchen.

One morning a ginger cat of about Moshie's own age called at the door. He peered over the curled edges of the iron bars that decorated the kitchen door and looked through the glass. He stood on his hind legs and Moshie Cat saw him.

He rose up slowly from the chair on which he was curled, stretched, unfolded himself, then loped over to the door.

They sniffed at each other with the glass pane

between them and then Moshie Cat pulled open the door with his claws and skipped out to greet the caller.

In a moment they had decided that they liked each other and when the ginger tom loped off towards the orchard Moshie Cat followed.

Before now he had never dared venture so far from his new home but, with the ginger cat's striped tail-tip waving before him, he forgot all his former timidity.

They romped among the thistles and the faded grass; dashed halfway up the trunks of the several huge pine trees that lined the road to throw themselves back to the earth; clambered among the neglected almond trees and sunned themselves on the tumbled-down walls which in hotter weather were the hunting ground of lizards.

Now the lizards lay in slumbering warmth, their quick bodies deep between the cracks in the stones; the almond trees were black and desolate, and the ground was awaiting the winter rains.

This friendship between the two young cats blossomed from the first moment. Every day the ginger tom poked his head round the door, almost at the same hour, and every day Moshie Cat was waiting for him.

With a slight mew of recognition he would jump up from the wicker chair and before he was out of the door the caller would be bounding away, leading him to their favourite playground.

The first ten days of January were traditionally splendid. The sunshine lingered until late afternoon and a tangle of forgotten roses bloomed in the deserted orchard. The branches of the almond trees were beginning to swell with sticky buds.

By this time Putchy had disappeared completely and never returned. Moshie Cat did not miss him and neither did the humans. They were rather relieved as, ultimately, he had grown decidedly vicious.

By the end of the month the orchard where the cats played was a vista of white blobs on the almond trees. It looked as though falling snowflakes had been caught on every twig, to be suspended there until they flushed pink and finally scattered the earth, thrown down by the new season's leaves.

The weather suddenly turned very cold. It rained for several days almost unceasingly and even when the skies cleared it did not grow warmer.

Everywhere was damp and uninviting and even the young cats seemed to have lost interest in playing in the orchard, whose soggy grasses clung to their flanks.

One afternoon the woman saw the ginger tom sitting miserably on top of the well. He was hunched up, his hair rubbed up the wrong way, and did not even move when the woman drew near. Usually he was very timid and dashed off at the first sight of any human.

Every now and then he opened his jaws wide, twisted his head uncomfortably and swallowed, and then he dipped his nose towards the water bucket and lapped with obvious pain.

Was it poison he had swallowed? Did he have

something stuck in his throat? How could anyone help a semi-wild creature that trusted no one?

The next morning he did not call on Moshie Cat as was his custom. Perhaps he had a home somewhere and was being looked after.

An icy wind blew and Moshie Cat stayed hunched on the wicker chair with no interest in going out.

To cut through the orchard, even though it was muddy, was a much quicker way of reaching the main road and when the woman went shopping the following day this was what she did. But she stopped short before she had crossed more than half of it.

Beside one of the broken walls was the ginger cat, his lively face frozen into a final snarl.

His only home had been the sun-hot summer walls and now they were cold and dripping with dampness. Moshie Cat had lost his winter friend.

That same afternoon Moshie Cat himself was obviously unwell. He began showing the same symptoms that his mistress had seen in the ginger cat, a difficulty in swallowing, the strained movement of the head, the anxiety for water and the pained manner of drinking.

He sat in his chair and looked very cross with himself, then he sat on the floor beside his water-bowl although it was chilly there.

As the day progressed he grew more and more unhappy and by nightfall was obviously ill. He was suddenly a rag, floppy and energyless, unless it was to open his mouth and twist his head.

'If he's not better by tomorrow I suppose you'd better find a vet to take him to,' said the man, which was rather astonishing for it was the first time he had shown any interest in Moshie Cat's existence.

Moshie Cat was definitely worse the following day so he was wrapped up in an old towel, pushed inside his owner's overcoat and taken to the mule-doctor in the village.

Even the car ride and the noises of the street, to which he was completely unaccustomed, did not stir him. His eyes were glazed and almost shut and his breath rasped heavily through his jaws.

His drunken face all crumpled, Moshie Cat was dying.

A wonderful thing happens

The vet was discovered in his favourite tavern, drinking black coffee and reading the morning newspaper. He glanced cursorily at the roughly furred body bulging out from the towel and was no doubt astonished that someone had actually bothered to bring him a cat.

'You'll have to come back later,' he said. 'My assistant isn't here at the moment.'

'Assistant? Won't I do?' said the woman.

'I shall have to give him an injection and you won't be able to hold him.'

This statement surprised the woman. Moshie Cat hardly had any life left in him and yet the man spoke as if a violent struggle would be forthcoming.

However, there was nothing to be done but wait. The vet had returned his gaze to the sports page and seemed to have forgotten the existence of his patient.

A couple of hours later the assistant arrived. He was a big fellow, accustomed to tackling pigs and mules and that roughly. The woman was almost afraid of leaving Moshie Cat in his hands.

The cat was stretched unresisting on the vet's desk, amid papers and inkpots. The assistant clamped strong hands over his back legs and the woman was asked to hold his head still, under the towel.

A needle was stuck in his haunch and Moshie Cat hardly winced when the antibiotic was injected. Then the woman gathered him in her arms again and wrapped him up.

'You must keep him warm,' said the vet. 'Don't let him go out or get wet. Keep him by the fire. And if you can wrap some old woolly about him all the better.'

'What's the matter with him anyway?'

The woman still half believed that he and his ginger playmate had eaten poison.

'Pneumonia,' said the vet. 'If he doesn't improve by tonight he won't get better.'

Moshie Cat was carefully watched all day. A big fire of olive logs was built up in the kitchen and a box was placed beside it for him to sleep in.

One of the children's old jerseys was cut down to his size and arranged about him as well as possible, tied with tapes to keep it from slipping, and a few spoonfuls of milk and brandy were forced down his throat from time to time.

Moshie Cat was almost unaware of all these efforts to save his life. His body was so heavy and yet, at the same time, it did not seem to be his at all.

There was coldness and greyness and pain, nothing more. Yet even the pain no longer seemed to belong to him.

The man came and stroked him. He picked him

up and nursed him in his arms, and this was a wonderful thing for he had never taken a cat in his arms before.

He rubbed his fingers through Moshie Cat's silky white underparts, knowing how much he loved this, but Moshie was aware of nothing.

He certainly seemed no different that night when the lights were put out. For the first time he did not sleep beside his mistress but stayed in the box which was pushed nearer to the slumbering ashes.

The stone hearth retained the fire's heat the whole night through and it was a warm place in which to sleep in the winter-time.

Moshie Cat was still alive the next morning. He was still very shaky and in no mood to eat. He dragged himself out of the box and trailed the jersey beneath him as he went outdoors.

He did not seem to have the sense to come back in again to the warmth, so he was picked up and brought back to the box. A new fire had been lighted, just for his benefit, for it was not really cold enough to merit one.

For the rest of the day he stayed unmoving in the box, returning gradually through rocking, swirling but tangible sensations, until he grew aware of the soft hissing of the logs and the heat that surrounded him.

He proceeded at once to pull himself out of the jersey, getting himself into a tangle and eventually wearing the woollen about his haunches instead of his chest. There was no doubt that he was getting better.

The children stroked him and Moshie Cat rubbed his ears against their hands, and when the man took him on his knees beside the fire while he read the newspaper, Moshie Cat began to purr.

The next few days were devoted to convalescence. It was a struggle to make Moshie Cat wear his jersey and, as the days were mild, it was eventually discarded.

He sat in the sun for half an hour or so, preening his white chest, and then he would return to the fireplace, there to doze for several hours.

His appetite also gradually returned and soon it was as if he had never been ill. His dull coat began to shine again and he purred with delight when the man cradled him in his arms and scratched him.

'I thought you didn't like cats,' accused the woman laughingly.

'Well I don't. But Moshie Cat's different. He's rather lovable and good-natured, even if he is so foolish. You can't help getting fond of him after a while.'

For such a confession from a cat-hater, Moshie Cat's pneumonia was almost worth while.

Moshie Cat goes exploring

As soon as Moshie Cat was sufficiently recovered from his illness to regather his growing sense of independence, he returned to his orchard playground.

His ginger friend had shown to him only a few of its many pleasures. Now it called to him insistently and he forgot the comfort of the warm fire, preferring to feel the wind blustering through his silky hair.

Perhaps at first he missed that dancing figure which had so often gone before him, hiding from him among the yellow thistles, pouncing out at him unexpectedly. But soon the thistles themselves were enough for him to play with.

The little girls would come to play in the orchard too. Moshie Cat watched them, sometimes coming up to pounce at their hands or lope behind their running legs.

As the time went by a lot of his fearfulness vanished. He was growing plump and sleek and was a kitten now only in his movements.

He would leave the house after his breakfast lick and polish and not return until the early afternoon gloom persuaded him.

When he saw the woman set off with her

shopping basket, the children beside her with dolls in their arms, dog-like he would follow.

He would not go out into the road but followed through all the neighbours' gardens, slipping under twisted wire fences, gliding through unchecked weeds, springing over the flowers.

When he could go no farther, checked by another road which crossed the one he followed, he would wait under a fallen pine tree, hiding among the rust-coloured needles until the people returned, the shopping completed.

Sometimes the woman would call to him and Moshie Cat would mew a short reply. In his eagerness he would run ahead, disappear for a while to reappear higher up the hill as if impatient at the slowness of his followers.

Usually he was sitting on the kitchen doorstep, calm and collected, long before the woman arrived there.

Then he would go off to the orchard, find a patch of sunlight where he would nibble the burrs out of his hair and lick himself into purring contentment.

Sometimes another cat strolled through Moshie's territory. They would sit staring patiently at each other until the intruder realized that his challenger was harmless and continued on his way.

Apart from these happenings, the time passed uneventfully until Moshie Cat was nearly a year old.

Spring was making the grass grow green and high, intermingled with the yellows, whites and violets of a myriad of wild flowers, and the branches of the almond trees were lost beneath the clustering foliage.

The hotel which bordered Moshie Cat's playground was also beginning to resound with voices and movements, after standing silently in the sun and rain all winter through.

This was a new discovery for Moshie Cat. He cautiously took up a comfortable situation on the wall which overlooked the hotel and spent a good many hours entertained by the things he saw there.

The hotel had been built on a much lower plane than the orchard and therefore Moshie Cat had a first-class view of everything.

He could see the terrace, the restaurant, the swimming-pool, as well as the gardens with their exotic plants and flowers, and the cars and taxis that passed up and down the drive right beneath him.

At first he was bewildered by the sight of so many people, and astonished when they began jumping in the unnaturally blue water and splashing about, but after a few days of watching these strange antics they no longer interested him.

What interested him more was the sight of Astor, running back and forth across the terrace as if it belonged to her, being patted by one stranger, called by another. She seemed to be enjoying herself greatly.

Moshie Cat came to the conclusion that if Astor could wander at will about the terrace, so could he.

So one day he gathered an immense amount of courage and went exploring.

He started in the back gardens, where no one ever went, not even Astor, but they were rather unexciting except for the birds that hopped about under the bushes, believing the place to be catless.

But Moshie Cat had already given up bird-catching as a waste of time, a hopeless business, and had more interesting things to occupy himself with.

It was not until the afternoon that, after much meandering and hesitation, Moshie Cat found himself at the foot of the wide stone steps that led up to the hotel terrace and swimming pool.

There was no one in sight. A silence has descended over the hotel's occupants. Those who were not at the beach were either asleep in their rooms or desultorily sunning themselves beside the swimming pool.

Moshie Cat glided up the steps, almost touching the wall. His view of the humans was quite different now. All he could see were lots of legs, or the occasional body stretched out on a bright-coloured mattress.

Curious, far too curious to turn back, Moshie Cat went on. It was not until the stairs were quite a long way behind him and the swimming pool was almost close, that he suddenly took fright.

Perhaps the unexpected movement of an arm, or the fall of a newspaper, startled him.

He suddenly dashed across the terrace as if who-knows-what terror chased behind him. Jumping a pair of naked feet, he streaked along the edge of the swimming pool and dived at last into the obscure refuge of some tall plants.

If the plants had not quivered, disclosing the presence of a stranger; if the owner of the feet had not been quite awake, the occupants of the terrace would not have believed their eyes.

The ones who were not asleep sat up and stared, exchanging remarks with their companions.

But although they looked about for several minutes, no one saw Moshie Cat eventually slink from his hiding place, reach the tall cemented wall and fling himself up it as only a cat knows how.

He did not stop trembling until he was back among the dandelions and the tangled grasses, from which sanctum that other world no longer seemed to exist.

A word about Stripes and an end to adventuring

If Stripes has not been mentioned very often in this part of the story it is because he was the kind of cat that blended so well with his surroundings that, although he existed, he remained for the most part quite unnoticed.

As soon as the almost telepathic communication reached him that Putchy would return to the house no more, Stripes took up his abode there.

He did this quite informally, with no fuss or bother. Nor did he ask permission. He just strolled nonchalantly into the kitchen one chilly morning, casually jumped up into what had been Moshie

Cat's favourite wicker chair, curled himself up and went to sleep.

From then on he lived in that chair. Every morning as soon as the kitchen door was opened to let Moshie Cat and the children out, Stripes strolled in.

He did not stir from the chair until the kitchen door was about to be locked at night and he was previously tipped out of it by the woman.

He nestled himself so firmly into the chair that not until its front was almost touching the floor, and he defying the laws of gravity, would he deign to admit that it was time to leave.

During the day he only moved from the chair if any food was thrown down for him outside the door. From the most somnolent state, he would flash down upon the morsel. As soon as it was swallowed, back he came and went to sleep.

Moshie Cat had no objection to his presence. Perhaps he too did not realize that Stripes existed,

for as soon as the tabby had settled himself into the chair he was utterly forgotten.

If Moshie Cat did happen to notice him there and mildly object, Stripes would growl fiercely, whereupon Moshie retreated.

Sometimes the man, who disliked Stripes intensely and threw him out whenever he happened to notice him, remonstrated with Moshie Cat for meekly accepting the intruder.

'You should turn him out,' he said. 'It's your home, not his. What's the use of a cat that lets all and sundry come through the door?'

Moshie Cat stared at the man, his yellow eyes blinking, and then he looked at the wall.

Now that he almost lived in the orchard, he was not very interested in what went on in the kitchen. He only came home at dusk and, if his mistress went out later on, grew very lonely.

He discovered that she went into the hotel and decided one day to follow her, nervously gliding down the staircase.

He found a big plant on the landing between the first and ground floors behind which he could hide and, at first, would go no farther than this. It was an interesting spot, from which he could spy on the movements of all those who passed by the reception desk or entered the lounge and dining-room.

Once he was persuaded into the lift by his mistress but the experience was so disturbing that he refused to repeat it. He preferred to trot up the stairs while his mistress used the lift, waiting for her where he knew she would appear.

On another occasion he found the courage to follow the man all the way down the stairs, across the reception and dining-room as far as the kitchen.

The cacophony, the blast of a dozen hot smells, was terrifying.

He fled alone along strange passages and hid for a while in the boiler room to regain composure before finding his own way up the back staircase, which led to the water tank beside his own kitchen door.

But these adventures into another world were quite enough for him. He made two or three trips more across the terrace, frightening himself each time by his own temerity, and then decided to leave it all to Astor.

The wild orchard, its almond trees budding with a new season's fruit; the locust-beans hanging in long green fingers; the grasshoppers sunning themselves on the wall; this was Moshie Cat's world, the one he knew, the kind he had been born into.

He satisfied his curiosity about the human's strange world by sitting on top of the wall and watching what was going on.

But more often, instead of watching the terrace and the swimming pool, his yellow eyes would take a downward bent towards the deserted back garden, where no humans wandered except an occasional gardener, and where the birds chattered fearlessly.

Which deals with rain and rabbits

On Moshie Cat's island it only rains about a dozen times a year. Therefore, when the sky does grow heavy with black clouds and the wind drops, the water comes down with a vengeance.

In one morning it must rain enough to suffice for a week somewhere else. Three hours of rain will flood the streets with rushing streams and block them with swirling mud.

In the village the houses echo with the music of water that rushes from the gutters, down the pipes inside the walls and into all the wells underneath.

There is nothing so precious as water on an island that has no natural rivers and where it hardly ever rains.

Everyone talks about how much water they have captured in their particular well and feels quite sorry when the sun begins to shine again.

Elenita and Kitty had two pet rabbits. They were only babies, hardly more than two months old.

One was sandy-coloured with a white streak on its nose. The other looked exactly like a wild rabbit, except for a patch of white on its shoulder. They were brother and sister.

It is fatal for rabbits to get their paws wet (at

least, so the natives say) so one May morning when the rain unexpectedly began to drench everything, all within the space of five minutes, they were hurriedly rescued from their hutch and brought into the house.

Moshie Cat watched with astonishment as the two baby rabbits tentatively sniffed and hopped and left their droppings about the sofa on which he was dozing. Never had such a thing happened before.

Knowing that they were 'untouchable' – his mistress had only two days beforehand introduced him to them as friends of the family – he hardly dared make close investigations.

Instead his ears pricked, his face grew into a frown, and the tip of his tail wagged ferociously.

Once, when the buck rabbit grew invitingly close, Moshie Cat was bold enough to tap at it with a paw. But his claws were sheathed and he did no harm.

The impertinent rabbit was completely unintimidated by Moshie Cat's size and smell. He hopped a pace closer and sniffed at the other's white breast, tickling with his quivering whiskers.

Moshie Cat sprang back with a start of fear and almost fell off the sofa.

He jumped on to the floor and the rabbit looked down at him, his floppy brown ears stiff with surprise.

A few minutes later the rabbits were banned from the sofa and the two children carried their respective pets into the kitchen.

'Let them hop around on the floor,' said the woman. 'As soon as it's dry you can take them out again.'

Moshie Cat sat in the kitchen doorway, his tail still flicking, his yellow eyes never leaving the playful little things.

They sniffed under the chairs, they frisked and jumped right under Moshie Cat's nose, and the buck rabbit suddenly went wild with the joy of so much space to hop about in. In half a dozen springs he was right across the kitchen.

His joy was short-lived, cut off in the middle of a hop.

Stripes, dozing in his chair, almost the colour of the wicker seat and completely forgotten as usual, had taken one huge spring and, with the quickest of movements, broke the rabbit's back.

He realized his mistake in the same moment that he had committed it, but it was too late.

While the rabbit twitched and cried he fled from cover to cover and eventually escaped into the rain.

Moshie Cat raced after him, as much frightened by the deed as if he himself had been the culprit.

After this there was no forgiving the humble tabby. He had already been excused several untoward robberies, including the theft of half a pound of cheese only two days earlier.

Astor was called in to keep him at bay and the fox-terrier had a marvellous time chasing after her old enemy whenever he was sighted.

She would look at the people with an expression

in her eyes which seemed to say, 'And about time you realized what an old sponger that cat is,' and joyfully raced after Stripes, barking frenetically, just as soon as she was called for this office.

With the passing of time the woman was inclined to pardon Stripes. He was growing rather thin. No doubt he had imagined, in his sleepy state, that the rabbit was some piece of food thrown for him.

But whenever she put forward the idea the children were adamant against it and Stripes was for ever banned.

It was not long after this, too, that they were to move again, so it was hardly worth encouraging the tabby to return.

They had rented another house in the village of Moshie Cat's birth and very soon everything was packed up and a lorry came to take the things away.

Moshie Cat kept well out of the way, dozing in his orchard or playing in the grass, filling his silky coat with burrs from the thistles.

He cried piteously and almost angrily from the basket into which he was tempted on his return, and crept out cautiously into an unknown and obscure little room, filled with books.

These he recognized by their smell and was somewhat comforted. Eventually he curled himself up on a pile of blankets in the corner and fell asleep.

The man's first words to his wife on returning to the village once again were, 'Now remember, no more cats.'

She faithfully promised that her heart was hardened. She would leave the cats to their respective fates and content herself with her favourite Moshie, whom everyone in the family had grown to love.

Interlude with half a dozen children

While Moshie Cat passed away the first lonely hours in his new home, sleeping on the blankets, Elenita and Kitty were sent to play with their ex-neighbours so that their mother could be left in peace to sort out the things that the men from the lorry had left in one big room.

Their ex-neighbours were, of course, Rafael, Manolita, Mari-Loli and Tomasin.

They were friendly enemies more than anything else and only tolerated each other's company for an hour or so before beginning to squabble and come to blows.

That summer afternoon things were rather tranquil. Tomasin had wandered off on his own and was somewhere among the neighbouring orchards; Rafael was reading a comic, and the two girls had brought out their dolls with which to entertain the visitors.

The time went by quite quickly in this fashion until Tomasin returned, carrying something in his grubby hands.

'Look what I've found,' he called out to the others gathered about the doorway of the house, in the shadow of a grape-vine.

They hardly took any notice until he broke into a

trot, fell, but did not let go of the thing he had found, though it made a vain spring from his grasp.

It was a tabby kitten, some five weeks old, and Tomasin had nearly pulled it to pieces for half an hour in the shade of someone's pomegranate tree.

He held it up by the tail and swung it in the faces of his sisters, causing them to scream with surprise and disgust.

'Ugh! What is it?' cried Manolita. 'Let me see.'

She stretched out her hands, but Tomasin was not giving up his prize so easily.

He dragged it out of her reach, then sat down with the small creature between his knees. While Manolita watched he began to pull its whiskers.

Elenita and Kitty drew close, watching him with serious faces.

Elenita said, 'Don't do that,' but Tomasin took no notice.

When Rafael came up and promised to punch him if he refused to hand over his find, Tomasin suddenly cried, 'It's a rat, it's a rat,' and threw it into his brother's face.

Rafael caught the refrain and tossed the kitten at his sisters, who screeched and ran.

'It's a rat, it's a rat,' squealed Tomasin again, grabbing it up and chasing after them.

For a while the kitten was tossed back and forth between them, hitting the ground, sailing through the air, until eventualy it fell into Elenita's hands.

She pulled it close to her, cradled it in her arms and refused to let it go.

After a while Tomasin said, 'Give it to me. It's mine. I found it.'

'No,' said Elenita. 'You're only going to hurt it.'

'It's mine,' shrieked the little boy and, as it looked as though he was about to bite (his favourite manner of getting his own way), Elenita began to run, the kitten still pressed against her chest.

At this moment her parents providentially appeared, strolling along the narrow pathway towards the house.

'Mama!' cried Elenita. 'Look what I've got.'

But her mother was disappointingly negative in her reaction. Elenita did not know that only that very afternoon she had promised to allow no more cats in the family.

'Tomasin is going to kill it if I leave it here,' she insisted desperately.

The woman began to weaken. She was remembering how Moshie Cat had come exhausted from the clutches of this same family.

But even while she hesitated, the man reminded

her, 'No more cats. We've only been here half a day.'

'Put it down somewhere. It probably belongs to someone,' suggested Elenita's mother and, not wanting to involve herself in the kitten's problem but at the same time feeling very guilty, she left the child to her own devices and went to look for Tomasin's mother.

Elenita had no intention of putting the kitten where Tomasin would quickly find it.

She kept on walking, feeling its warmth through the thinness of her dress, until she came to the little green car that belonged to her father.

She opened the door, dropped the kitten behind the back seat, then hurried back to her parents. The kitten was not mentioned again.

As soon as they got home, however, Elenita pulled it from its hiding place and triumphantly carried it into the house.

'Isn't he sweet?' she said. 'He looks just like Putchy. Mama, please don't say we can't keep him. He's only very little.'

Relating to Putchy the Second

For two days Putchy the Second hovered on the borders of life. He spent them in the fireplace, where he was put to be out of the way, his energy gradually seeping away.

He had eaten some food but it had done him no good and it seemed as though he only wanted to die, unmolested by anyone.

Not even the woman had time to notice him much, for still the house was in a chaotic state with toys and trunks and chairs all over the place, and Elenita and Kitty were busy exploring the new garden.

In the evening, when at last the children were in bed and the woman could relax for a while, she picked up the little tabby. It was half frozen, far nearer to death than life.

She forced some milk and brandy down its throat then wrapped it up in a duster and put it back in the box that had been found for it.

Moshie Cat came in from his first investigations in the garden, went stiff all over at the sight and smell of a new feline, and fled out of doors again.

There were plenty of things to see and smell. The garden was full of fruit trees, but they were too small and slender for him to climb except the apricot, the quince and the pomegranate.

The last two were to become his favourites, the quince because it led to the top of the wall that overlooked a street at the foot of the garden, the pomegranate because its top branches were always filled with birds.

On the first evening in his new haunt Moshie Cat did no more than sharpen his claws on the trunk of the pomegranate tree and sniff about the pens where the rabbits had been put and where pigs and chickens had once known shelter.

When at last he returned to the kitchen, the sky now dark and broken with masses of stars, he did not even remember the kitten wilting away in the fireplace.

He slunk about the new rooms, played with a leaf that had fluttered in through the french windows and decided that the plants that decorated the biggest room saved him the necessity of going out to the garden when nature called.

It took him at least two weeks to learn that this was not so and meanwhile he almost uprooted the plants from their pots. Luckily they were hardy and survived.

The night was very long and very hot but Putchy the Second grew colder.

Moonlight flooded the silent house and at two in the morning the woman woke up. She was unable to sleep any more and, remembering the kitten, decided to see how it was getting on.

Moshie Cat ran down the stairs beside her and

slipped out to the garden. He began to play among the lilies and forgot about sleep.

In the kitchen the woman was forcing more warm milk and brandy between the kitten's jaws. It was stiff with cold now and she felt sure that before the sun arrived it would be dead.

But cats do not die so easily, not even very little ones.

The whole of the next day Putchy the Second lay unmoving in the fireplace, except when the woman picked him up two or three times to dose him as before.

Elenita was anxious as her mother had told her to expect the worst. Moshie Cat was hostile and hissed whenever he saw the kitten.

By nightfall, however, Putchy the Second suddenly staggered to all fours and rushed upon the plate from which Moshie Cat was fastidiously feeding.

He growled ferociously, frightening Moshie into surrendering the whole plateful, and attacked the big chunks of meat with a rage of hunger. So small that he had to climb into the plate itself, he snarled and dribbled but could not get even one piece into his mouth.

Moshie Cat watched the performance with amazement but did not dare to draw near.

The woman hurriedly cut up some more meat into small pieces and had to use force to drag the kitten away from Moshie Cat's dish before pushing its nose into the other.

Moshie Cat looked on while the kitten slavered

over the small plate, washing down the meat afterwards with a saucer of milk.

Then he went back to his own dish but, before he could get into it again, the kitten was a second time intruding, stealing it from under his nose.

Eventually the bloated Putchy had to be put outside so that Moshie Cat could finish his supper in peace, a long process, for he never hurried.

When Moshie Cat went out to the garden the kitten sprang upon him, sinking his tiny teeth into the other's haunch and causing him to howl.

He sprang away, shooting into the branches of the lemon tree for safety, and from this undignified retreat watched the kitten play with its tail.

Moshie Cat remembers how to play

It took Moshie Cat at least a fortnight to accustom himself to Putchy the Second. Used to lazing about alone in the sunshine of the orchard, he had grown slothful and forgotten his kittenish ways.

Putchy the Second reminded him.

There was never a moment when Moshie Cat was not startled by needle-like teeth suddenly crunching into his tail, or a small body flinging itself upon his back.

He would be sniffing through the long grass beneath the plum trees when out of it would pounce the writhing tabby kitten. His heart would pound and he would flee up the grape-vine to safety.

Gradually Moshie Cat was reminded of the games he used to play and soon the two animals were chasing each other all over the house and garden.

When Moshie Cat tired he always had his escape, up into the trees or vines, where Putchy the Second tried in vain to follow him. He was still far too small.

In the big room Moshie Cat would hide behind the huge plant pot, which was itself lost beneath the overflowing leaves of its occupant, and wait for the other to wander unexpectedly in.

Their bodies could be heard thudding on the tiles, the rocking-chairs creaked madly back and forth as they played a furious game of catch, and the leaves of the plants shook as if caught in a high wind.

There were howls and growls and whipping tails.

In the end it was necessary to ban them from the house in order to save the indoor plants from irreparable damage. Moshie Cat was called in at night-time and Putchy the Second was firmly pushed outside.

This took up at least half an hour every night, especially when he was older. He would hide under chairs, cling to table legs, jump in again through open windows.

The woman was adamant. The two cats could not share the house at night. They began their games at four in the morning, charging across beds, thundering underneath them, wrestling on top of the sleeping children and invariably waking up everybody.

By midday both of them were asleep in the sunshine, curled into each other on top of an old wooden chest. Had they not been of different colours, it would have been difficult to know where one cat ended and the other began, so intermingled were their legs and tails.

Putchy the Second was not very popular with the humans in the house, except for his saviour Elenita.

When he was not playing and sleeping he was looking for something to eat and the older he got the greedier he became.

Never was there a cat so well fed and yet so constantly in search of food. It became his life's work. Even Fatty could not have kept pace with him.

He would eat up his own portion then steal what he could from Moshie Cat. This would have been the whole plateful had not the woman kept him forcefully at bay. Moshie Cat was too timid to protect his own interests.

If he could find the paper that the meat had been wrapped in, he would eat that too.

He sniffed all about the rubbish box, just like the starving village cats, and kept the pigeons from the household scraps thrown down for them by eating them himself, this even when the scraps were lettuce and tomato.

By the time he was six months old he did nothing all day long except sit by the refrigerator or follow the woman about while she prepared the meals, constantly mewing about her legs and making a great nuisance of himself.

He was a past master at the art of getting himself inside the larder and did not mind how many hours he was locked in, even though most of the food kept there was in tins or packets.

Putchy the Second and the man of the house felt a mutual aversion to each other from the first moment and would never share a room.

Elenita was his only defender. She loved him, nursed him, insisted that he should not be left out when any scraps went begging, and was very indignant when it was suggested that he was already overfed.

The garden in this new home was completely enclosed and it was difficult for strange cats to enter. Those that did were not encouraged.

Only one was persistent, a black she-cat who was so bold that she would enter the house itself, steal what she could and nonchalantly stroll out again.

Moshie Cat would watch her but give no warning of her approach. Putchy the Second chased after her, wanting to play, or perhaps wanting to share her spoils.

War was declared against this particular animal, so defiant, so cunning and so cool.

In eight months every kind of missile was thrown at her – stones, logs, oranges, brushes, shoes – but she had such a way of twisting around the tree-trunks, putting them between herself and her pursuer, that she invariably escaped unharmed.

The man talked threateningly of borrowing a shotgun or setting a trap, but these ideas were abandoned as too risky. The black she-cat is probably boss of the garden to this day.

Apart from this almost daily attack on the black cat, life was very tranquil in Moshie Cat's new home. When he was bored he watched the rabbits, numerous now, or half-heartedly chased after the pigeons, although their flapping wings frightened him.

He crouched in the pomegranate tree watching the birds, unable to reach the highest branches where they perched and squabbled.

He watched Putchy the Second rummaging for rubbish, filling his whiskers with fluff. He watched the children at play.

When the woman planted any new flowers Moshie Cat watched with interest then later would go and dig them up.

He liked to sit in the big plant pots, regardless of the plant squashed uncomfortably underneath him, and could not understand why the woman got cross with him.

When wire netting was fixed over the best of them Moshie Cat sat on top of that. Except for grass, weeds and rabbits, little flourished in the new garden.

Moshie Cat kills a rat

Moshie Cat was lonely when his mistress went away for a week. The children had gone away, too, and the house and garden were unnaturally silent.

He was not much happier when she came back. She brought with her a strange creature that took up so much of her time that Moshie Cat felt rather ignored.

The new addition to the household was a baby. Moshie Cat was picked up by the woman and introduced to this very small human being, but he still could not quite make up his mind what it was.

It mewled just like a tiny kitten, causing him to prick his ears and pull himself up on to the pram wheels, trying to see what was inside the pram.

Putchy the Second immediately realized that the pram would be a very comfortable place in which to sleep. He quickly installed himself and was just as quickly removed – at least ten times.

Moshie Cat also tried out the new sleeping place but the woman was so cross when she found him there that he decided not to make a habit of it.

He ran out to the garden and found a sunny spot on top of one of the plants. The woman was cross again and chased him away from there, too. In the end he ran up on to the roof of the outhouse and watched the pigeons.

As the weeks went by Moshie Cat spent more and more time in the trees and on the roofs and only returned to the kitchen at night when the garden was invaded by darkness and damp chills.

Putchy the Second mewed to be let in and tore ferociously at the door, certain that he was being left out of something eatable.

Moshie Cat sat by the fire among the airing nappies and watched the woman with the baby in her arms. Before, the evenings had been for him. Now she was always with this small creature.

Once he tried to jump on to her lap while the baby was there. There was room for him but, at the last moment, he changed his mind. But already he was in mid-air.

He twisted about, lost balance and landed right on the baby's face, digging one claw into its cheek as he took off again.

The resultant howls discouraged him from ever again trying to share the woman's lap with the baby.

Upstairs in the bedroom the baby's cot was very warm. Each time Moshie Cat was found in it he was pulled out. But for once he was stubborn. He liked sleeping in the small cot with its new blankets and hot-water bottle.

So, for the first time, he found himself banned from the bedroom at night. This was no great discomfort as he curled up comfortably in the

fireplace, where the wood ash kept its heat till
morning.

When Putchy the Second came scratching at the
french windows Moshie Cat ran into the big room
and called to him.

Sometimes the black renegade cat came to peer
at him, alone in the moonlit darkness, and Moshie
Cat scratched at the windows, trying to get out.

Eventually Moshie Cat did not answer when the
woman called him in at night. He preferred to be
outside, sharing the darkness with the other cats.
There was a world in the midnight garden that he
had not yet discovered.

How lively were the rabbits in the silent hours, quivering and stretching their tall ears to catch every sound. The pigeons broke their slumber to coo and quarrel, and the fallen leaves moved when insects passed by underneath them.

A baby rabbit escaped from the old hutch beneath the grape-vine. Putchy the Second was on it in a moment and spent the rest of the night eating it, growling at Moshie Cat to keep him at bay.

Crouched in the pomegranate tree, Moshie Cat watched strange cats slink across the garden. The lizards did not come out of their holes in the cold weather but he watched the moonlit walls with pricked ears, just in case.

One night, when winter was almost over, Moshie Cat sensed fear among the rabbits. They were very still, crouched together in one corner of the old hen-run.

Their gaze was fixed upon a dark creature that had come from a hole in the wall. Moshie Cat went stiff all over. It was a half-grown rat that he smelled.

For a moment he was afraid, but some instinct compelled him to investigate.

In so many games had he stalked an imaginary enemy that the rat knew nothing of his approach until he was up against the wire netting, trying to find an entrance.

Startled, the rat shot across the rabbit run, found a hole and, all within a second, was fleeing round the garden wall, looking for refuge.

Moshie Cat chased after him. Fear had gone, replaced by the hunter's instinct.

Cornered, the rat reared on to its hind legs and chattered with rage. At its back was the trunk of the vines, but it dared not climb it with the cat so close.

Moshie Cat tentatively pawed at his enemy, but drew back at the rat's hissing frenzy. He tried to circle about it and take it unawares, but the rat's red-rimmed eyes followed his every movement.

Putchy the Second was up on the garden wall, sniffing for night insects. At that moment he decided to find out what was going on down below.

He came gingerly down the slim trunk of the vine, halted at the sight of the rat which was making short lunges with its head at Moshie Cat, and hissed sharply.

The rat looked up and in the same second was bowled over by Moshie Cat's sudden spring. It got away, tail stiff in the air, but now there were two cats after it and there was no escape.

Moshie Cat pounced again, recovered as he felt the rat slip way, and yet a third time sunk his claws into his prey.

The rat whipped about, tail writhing, feet scrabbling, squealing with fear and pain.

Then suddenly it was silent and still and now it was Moshie Cat's turn to growl, warning the excited Putchy that this affair had nothing to do with him.

He did not eat the rat. He carried it to the french windows and put it down beside a plant pot. He spent the rest of the night crouched beside it, now and again pulling at it with a claw, and jumped up with a mew of delight when the woman came to open the kitchen door.

Moshie Cat pulled the rat along by its nose and left it at the woman's feet, his yellow eyes blinking as he looked up at her.

He purred with joy when she picked him up and scratched him all over, then suddenly sprang from her arms to chase after the pigeons that were fluttering down from their perches.

Now that the rat had been handed over and appreciated, he had quite forgotten it.

He was galloping among the pigeons with a stiff tail, and just as suddenly stopped his frolics to sharpen his claws on the bark of the orange tree.

Farewell to Moshie Cat
and his island

The people were moving again and this time the cats could not go with them. They were leaving the island to take up residence in a small flat in a big city.

Moshie Cat, used to his orchards and his trees, unaware of the existence of traffic, terrified of men, could only be unhappy there.

Putchy the Second, who liked to roam his neighbours' rooftops and delve into their rubbish, would be just as lost.

Elenita cried, and the woman tried to convince herself that she could live without Moshie Cat. Even the man said, 'I suppose we can't really take him with us?'

But what was to be done with them? They could not be entrusted with a neighbour, who would soon forget to care for them, and they had certainly never learned to care for themselves (although it was agreed that Putchy the Second would soon learn the laws of survival).

There is only one place on Moshie Cat's island where ownerless cats can live free from fear and hunger, only one place where they could be happily left. It is the Animal Refuge on the Valldemosa Road.

Two days before the people were to go away, a basket was put down in the garden for the cats to sniff about in. They found it very exciting, full of the scents of unknown dogs and cats, and almost fought over whom it should belong to.

Moshie Cat slept in it first, then Putchy the Second took his turn, but when it came to putting them both in together they were up in the trees and with every intention of staying there.

Moshie Cat knew all about moving by now and had been suspicious for several days. Putchy the Second sensed his companion's unrest and was guided by it.

Eventually they were coaxed into the house, but not into the basket, to which they had taken a violent dislike all of a sudden.

Putting two cats into one basket is like trying to catch five eggs with two hands. One always escaped. Tempers, both feline and human, were very much frayed by the time the lid was shut down and the bolt pushed home.

The cats growled and hissed and the basket shook. It shook all the fifteen miles to the Animal Refuge and Moshie Cat sounded very, very cross.

When at last the journey was over and the lid was lifted, Putchy the Second shot out like a jack-in-the-box. His tail looked like a fox's brush. He immediately hid himself behind a row of sleeping-boxes among some bushes and prowled about for some time, gradually deflating himself.

Moshie Cat was not so easily calmed. He too had thrown himself from the basket. Finding himself in a strange garden, full of cats and boxes, he was utterly panic-stricken.

He fled to a high wall and made a number of desperate leaps, trying to scale it. He dashed to a pair of tall wooden gates, topped with wire netting, and tried vainly to leap over these too.

He ran hither and thither, back and forth, then disappeared into a small, shadowy yard.

In the yard was a low shed. Moshie Cat sprang on to its roof, searching anxiously for the next leaping point, but there was none. There was only a big box, half hidden behind a sack.

Moshie Cat pushed his head inside it. It smelled of cats and he was suspicious. He sniffed all round, his whiskers tickled by the thick straw bed it contained.

Then he went right inside, for it was warm and dark and comforting.

He had not been there very long when he heard a voice that he knew. The woman was beside the box, calling him.

'Moshie . . . Moshie . . .'

Moshie Cat poked his head out. He pricked his ears and stared at the woman. How bewildered were his big yellow eyes in that moment.

'Why am I here?' they seemed to say. 'What is this?'

The woman repeated his name several times and then she went away.

Moshie Cat stayed for some time in the box he had found for himself. His heart no longer beat quite so madly. He had almost forgotten that he had not found the new box in his own garden.

After a while he decided to explore. Cautiously he crept out of the little yard and before him again was the big garden.

There were cats everywhere, big ones, little ones, and of every colour imaginable. A dog with a bandaged leg limped among them but none of the cats seemed to mind.

All about the garden, too, were wooden boxes covered with green plastic. Every box was stuffed with straw and Moshie Cat sniffed his way into several of them. They all smelled of cats.

At every few paces there was a plateful of food, milk or water. Moshie Cat nibbled at a sardine, then, wandered over to another plate that smelled of chicken but he was still not happy enough to feel hungry.

He meandered right across the garden. Other cats looked at him lazily but did not challenge his right of way. Most of them were dozing.

He passed an open brick shed outside which three separate litters of kittens were playing, watched by their respective mothers.

Another dog ambled by. Moshie Cat went stiff all over but the dog did not even look at him.

Eventually he halted on the outskirts of a wilderness. Bushes and trees grew everywhere. There were no boxes or shelters here, only dandelions and thorns and a few yellow roses.

A high wall threw a shadow over the whole area and Moshie Cat's hairs stood on end. Instinct warned him against venturing here but curiosity compelled him to continue his investigations.

He slunk under the bushes and came face to face with a skinny grey cat that glared at him. It hissed and shot out a tearing claw, only just missing the intruder's nose.

Hurriedly Moshie Cat backed away, so hurriedly that he bumped into a tabby she-cat curled up half asleep under a pine branch. She too sprang up and hurled herself upon him.

He dashed back to the brightness and the frolicking kittens. Never again did he pass the dividing line between the wild cats that inhabited the shadowy jungle and the domestic cats that dwelt in the garden. He saw Putchy the Second, swollen with food but still mulling over a plate of milk, completely adapted to his new surroundings.

Moshie Cat sat in the sunlight and watched him for a while, his eyes blinking. Then he began to wash himself.

Piccolo Fiction

True Adventures and Picture Histories

Colour Books and Fiction

COLOUR BOOKS

Great new titles for boys and girls from eight to twelve. Fascinating full-colour pictures on every page. Intriguing, authentic easy-to-read facts.

DINOSAURS   Jane Werner Watson
SECRETS OF THE PAST   Eva Knox Evans
SCIENCE AND US   Bertha Morris Parker
INSIDE THE EARTH
Rose Wyler and Gerald Ames
EXPLORING OTHER WORLDS
Rose Wyler and Gerald Ames
STORMS   Paul E. Lehr
SNAKES AND OTHER REPTILES
George S. Fichter
AIRBORNE ANIMALS   George S. Fichter

25p each   Fit your pocket – Suit your purse

FICTION

For younger readers
ALBERT AND HENRY
Alison Jezard   20p
ALBERT IN SCOTLAND
Alison Jezard   20p

Piccolo Book Selection

PUZZLES AND GAMES